Rom i:16
Bill Burger
2009

DEATH AMONG THE CYPRESS KNEES

DEATH AMONG THE CYPRESS KNEES

A Mark Garrison Mystery

Bill Burgett

iUniverse, Inc.
New York Lincoln Shanghai

Death among the Cypress Knees

A Mark Garrison Mystery

iUniverse books may be ordered through booksellers or by contacting:

iUniverse
2021 Pine Lake Road, Suite 100
Lincoln, NE 68512
www.iuniverse.com
1-800-Authors (1-800-288-4677)

This is a work of fiction. All of the characters, names, incidents, organizations, and dialogue in this novel are either the products of the author's imagination or are used fictitiously.

ISBN: 978-0-595-44418-2 (pbk)
ISBN: 978-0-595-88747-7 (ebk)

Printed in the United States of America

CHAPTER 1

▼

"What are cypress knees?" Sarah asks no one in particular from the back seat. Apparently, she has peeked at my transfer orders from the USDA Forest Service, so her question doesn't surprise me. I've been reassigned to Louisiana to investigate a possible homicide. The naked body of an unidentified girl has been found among the cypress knees in a swamp near Kisatchie National Forest.

"They're roots of a bald cypress tree."

"They have a weird name."

"They're called knees because they stick out of the water and are bent like knees. Since the rest of the roots are under water, the knees keep the tree alive by exchanging gases. Some people cut them off."

"Why?"

"Because the wood is very hard, and when it's polished it makes beautiful decorative pieces."

My transfer orders didn't come as a surprise to me. I have more experience in law enforcement than most rangers, having served in both military and civilian police forces—just what the Forest Service needs for a possible homicide investigation. Although still in good physical shape at 44, I'm ready for a move from the Appalachian Trail to flatter terrain.

The orders are less propitious for Lauren, my new wife, and her daughter, Sarah. When Lauren and I should be going on a honeymoon, we're being transferred to Louisiana. A former deputy sheriff from Littleton, New Hampshire, Lauren understands the need to investigate a possible homicide while the evidence is fresh; on the other hand, she's waited a long time for a honeymoon.

It's been several years since my pregnant wife, Judy, was killed in an explosion at an abortion clinic. She and our pastor, Donna Kraft, were about to meet with the abortionist to protest his activities. While waiting outside the clinic to take her home, I saw and heard the explosion that killed Judy and seriously injured the pastor. Judy and I knew that getting involved in the abortion issue was risky. To my regret I did little to dissuade her.

Judy taught me much about life. With her I was overcoming the emotional handicap of being raised in a dysfunctional family. She helped me expand my range of emotions. With her I learned how to laugh and cry—then came the explosion. Afterwards, I reverted to living in my head.

Deputy Sheriff Lauren Adams and I worked as part of a team assigned to find the person who blew up the clinic. Over time we discovered that we had much in common. She, too, was raised in a difficult family situation, her mother having died when she was five. Like me, she started her career in the military, which she left when she became pregnant with Sarah. Now, Lauren is giving me another chance at life. She waited patiently for me to recover from Judy's death before springing her marriage trap. She wants this marriage to be about us. I've made a promise to myself that I'll keep this family safe.

Lauren's father, Arthur Adams, whom everyone knows as Ace, is a retired contractor. Years of home building have leathered his hands and weathered his face. He looks older than his sixty one years. Even tempered, carefully groomed for over twenty years by the same barber, and bespectacled, Ace is only comfortable in a flannel shirt, denim pants, and half-boots. Raised by thrifty, conservative, God-fearing parents, Ace demands fairness and honesty in himself and others. His wife, Cora, Lauren's mother, whom he courted for three years before they married, died of breast cancer six years afterwards. Although never a smoker because of his love of outdoor sports, Ace developed a passion for beer after Cora's death. Good sense led him to enter a recovery program, and he's been a sponsor for many recovering alcoholics. He's also been the primary caregiver for Sarah. Lauren and Sarah are his whole life. Sage advice and patience have kept Sarah on the straight and narrow in a teenaged world full of detours. Ace is, in fact, the only male authority figure Sarah has known in her nuclear family until I happened along. Widowed when Lauren was five, Ace ran his contracting business and raised Lauren by himself, then retired and became a live-in grandpa to Sarah.

Thirteen is not a good age for Sarah to move. Changing middle schools near the end of the school year can be difficult, especially when there is a boy friend involved. We may as well be moving to China. To complicate matters, she has a new, utterly inexperienced father figure in her life. Lauren and I weighed the possibilities of leaving her in New Hampshire with her grandfather, but Lauren persuaded me that at this stage of her life Sarah needs her mother. Lauren decided to be a stay at home mom in Louisiana as long as necessary. There was little reaction when we told Sarah about the move. She had seen the transfer orders.

Millie Disch and Judy served together on the pro-life committee of our church. After Judy's death, Millie opened her farm house to unmarried expectant mothers as an alternative to abortion. She also opened her kitchen to a grieving forest ranger; thus, we became good friends. She's like a mother to me. An independent, seventy-ish farm woman, Millie will adjust to my move. She's a survivor, having already outlived three husbands. After selling my chalet in the White Mountains, I purchased her farm, leased the acreage, and employed a hand so that she'll no longer be burdened by daily chores. Millie may continue to live in the old farm house for as long as she likes, and can now spend more time in her flower garden, or reading Agatha Christie mysteries. Besides, with me gone she won't be tempted to play detective, although without her 12 gauge "Annie Oakley," it's doubtful we'd have captured the man responsible for Judy's death.

Whether untimely or not, we've accepted our transfer to Louisiana and are prepared for the consequences. We have no idea what that will mean.

"There it is," Lauren says, pointing to a brown sign reading "Natchez Trace Parkway." We turn in the direction of the arrow and enter the 444-mile national park linking Nashville, Tennessee, and Natchez, Mississippi. The trace is the last major leg of our journey from New England to the Gulf.

Our first stop on the trace is the Visitor's Center where we purchase narration tapes for the historic trip. Sarah buys a postcard to send to her boy friend back home. I've always had a fascination with history and nature and an aversion to surprise, so I studied the trace before we left. It's a natural pathway carved by animals and Native Americans over many centuries. In the eighteenth and early nineteenth centuries it was the way north for tradesmen who floated their goods down the Mississippi to the Gulf of Mexico. Because it wasn't possible then to navigate the Mississippi northward against its current, these hardy adventurers hiked home by way of the trace, their pockets bulging with money. Most were lucky enough to survive the elements and the outlaws. The trace, however, is littered with the bones of the unlucky.

Over the centuries the Natchez Trace has been the chosen route of such notable men as Hernando DeSoto, John Audubon, Andrew Jackson, and Abraham Lincoln. A memorial stands at the burial place of explorer Meriwether Lewis whose violent death on the trace is still a cold case. Since 1812, when the first steamboat paddled and bellowed its way upstream, the trace has been retired as the only way back home. Recognizing its place in history, the government constructed the Natchez Trace Parkway in the early 1930's. It's a national treasure.

No one speaks as we enter the 50 miles-per-hour two-lane road. The manicured landscape and absence of commercial traffic is a terrific relief after the stress of driving for two days on the interstate highways. Lauren is a native New Englander. She's never been in the Deep South, not to mention the Deep South in April. We suffer the cool air blowing through open windows so that we can enjoy the scents and sights of the spring flower show. Camellias, azaleas, and magnolias are bursting forth in their magnificence. Lauren is not usually given to outbursts, so when she yells for me to stop I'm certain that we're in imminent danger. Only after she jumps from the car with camera in hand do I regain my composure.

The narration tapes use mile markers to locate historical sites and roadside services. Because my Excursion doesn't have a built-in cassette player, Sarah serves as audio engineer, using her portable tape player. She's good at the task, interrupting whatever is happening to announce the next important milestone. Lauren, understanding her daughter's short attention span, is delighted that she takes the task so seriously. We worried that an unspoken resentment about leaving New Hampshire might shut her down. Our fears are not entirely unfounded.

"Have they ever heard of ballet in Louisiana?" Sarah asks her mother.

"Of course they have."

"Can I take lessons again?"

"We'll find a studio as soon as we get there."

"And what if there isn't one?"

"There will be," Lauren promises, watching for an expression on my face. I know that she has no idea whether there's a ballet studio in Natchitoches, Louisiana.

Sarah is a budding ballerina, who's kept herself in trim at 110 pounds, five feet four inches. Although she stands straight, walks with grace, and is remarkably pretty, she's every bit a prototypical teenager. Her natural hair color is brown, but now it's tinted auburn, possibly to differentiate herself from her mother. She's individualizing, Lauren tells me. Lauren and Ace insist that Sarah not be tattooed and that piercings be restricted to two per ear—that's that. Her most distinctive feature is her smile, slight dimples included. It's dental-perfect without orthodontic assistance. She's thirteen, going on sixteen, as they say. Her choice of music bugs the adults in her life. As of the moment her favorite is hip-hop—a mixture of rap music and break dancing which seems to me like just so much bad poetry set to beat. Nevertheless, as long as it's benumbed by a headset, Lauren copes. Ace merely retreats to the comfort of his recliner. I'm a latecomer to this scene, so I keep quiet.

"Who are you calling?" Lauren asks Sarah.

"Grandpa."

"You miss him, don't you?" Sarah gives her mother the "duh" look.

"Hello, Grandpa. This is Sarah. We're on the Natchez Trace Parkway and I'm the sound technician. We have tapes that tell about the trace. My job is to tell Mark when to stop at historical places. Where are you now? What are you up to?" … "I'm sorry. Want me to call back?" … "I miss you, too, Grandpa. Will you ever come to visit us?" … "I have to go. We're coming to one of the places where the parkway crosses the original trace. Mark wants to see it. I'll call you tomorrow. I love you, Grandpa. Say hello to Mrs. Disch." Hanging up, she announces the upcoming marker.

"Is Grandpa with Mrs. Disch?" Lauren asks.

"Were you listening?"

"It's hard not to in the car, honey. I'm sorry."

"It's okay, I guess. Yes, he's with Mrs. Disch. They're playing backgammon."

"I'm glad they're together."

"I guess."

"You don't sound glad, Sarah. Is there something wrong?"

"No."

Lauren and I exchange glances. It's bad enough that Sarah's been forced to leave her friends, including her boy friend, but the developing friendship between Ace and Millie Disch may be hard for Sarah to take.

The two day drive along the Natchez Trace Parkway ends in Natchez, Mississippi, on the big river. We spend two days there; barely time enough to see the king cotton antebellum mansions and the notorious Natchez-under-the-Hill where men like legendary outlaw John Murrell squandered their plunder on whisky and prostitutes. On the last night before our westward turn onto U.S. 84, our newly formed family dines at Mammy's Cupboard, enjoying our first truly southern cuisine, ending with coconut pie. As dessert is served, I propose a toast to my new family, "To the beginning of a wonderful life together." Sarah's gaze never lifts from her plate. Lauren and I vow to return to Natchez for a more relaxed vacation.

We begin the final leg of our journey to Natchitoches before the sun comes up. Lauren sleeps and Sarah gazes out the window with her headset in place. My mind begins to focus on what's ahead.

Although Lauren and Sarah know that a young woman was found dead in a cypress swamp, they don't know that she wasn't the first. Another young woman was found dead in the same swamp a year before. I don't want to start our marriage with secrets, but this is more than they need to know. I'd have preferred to come alone, and then return to New Hampshire, but I know that Lauren would have none of that, and it isn't consistent with my transfer orders. I shoot an arrow prayer, "Lord, protect us from all danger," then turn the Excursion west.

The first order of business in Louisiana is to get Sarah back in school. "You know Sarah's coming in near the end of the school year," the assistant principal tells us.

"We didn't pick April. My husband was transferred by his employer," Lauren replies.

"I'd like for Sarah to meet with the guidance counselor to determine her class placement," the assistant principal says, standing and looking at Sarah. "You can wait here, Mr. and Mrs. Garrison. I'll be right back." He motions for Sarah to follow.

"Whatever," Sarah says, leaving the room.

Returning alone, the assistant principal sits in a chair in front of his desk and faces Lauren. "It isn't easy for a student to transfer, especially at this time."

"This time?" Lauren asks.

"She's probably going to be placed in the eighth grade, the last year of our middle school program. Most of the other students have been together for several years, some since kindergarten. They've created social bonds. You're also going to find that her curriculum may be different than what she left on the East Coast, meaning that she could be at a different level in some core courses. She'll either have to catch up or do busy work. We aren't staffed to provide individual tutoring."

"That's only part of Sarah's challenge," Lauren says. "Ranger Garrison and I were just married. She left behind a grandfather who has been a father figure for her since she was five, and a boyfriend that she has grown fond of over the past year. She has a lot of reasons for not wanting to be here."

"Why didn't you leave her where she was at least until the school year ended?"

"It was a hard decision, but I believe that she needs me at this age."

"You'll have to provide close supervision and encouragement. Are you going to work outside the home?"

"No, at least not for awhile. I left a position as a deputy sheriff in New Hampshire and I want to remain active in law enforcement, but for now I'm going to help my husband and Sarah get acclimated, then we'll see."

The guidance counselor appears at the door with Sarah and announces, "Sarah is well prepared for the eighth grade. She may need some advanced assignments in mathematics since her former program is further along than ours is. I believe that we can arrange that." Turning to Sarah, the counselor says, "Sarah, welcome. I'm glad you're here. We'll do all we can to make you feel comfortable."

"Thank you," Sarah says halfheartedly.

The assistant principal goes over a sheet listing enrollment requirements with Lauren, then extends his hand to each of us. "Assuming that you have everything on this list at the beginning of the day tomorrow, we'll get Sarah started. Welcome to Louisiana and don't hesitate to call on me if you have any questions."

As we leave the school, busses are lining up to load. With the student's eyes focused on Sarah, she breaks away and runs to the Excursion, but the doors are locked. Lauren scrambles for her keys and unlocks the doors as we hurry to catch up. When we get to the SUV, Sarah is sobbing in the front seat. Lauren reaches out to her but she turns away, and we ride to our unfurnished apartment in silence.

The Department of Agriculture, host of the National Forest Service, provides a modest moving allowance for rangers. Although I have some furniture at the farm house, Millie still lives there, and Ace lives in Lauren's house, so Lauren and I pieced together what furniture our houses could spare and hired a moving company to bring it to Louisiana. It was agreed that the furniture would be here when we arrived, but the truck got bogged down somewhere in Tennessee with transmission problems. Our furniture is waiting to be transferred to another truck. All we can do is wait in the empty apartment, so we decide to make our time count. I beat the girls repeatedly in three-deck solitaire.

The apartment is one of two in a duplex built in the sixties. Well maintained and freshly painted, it's all we need until we have a better vision of the future. Built in a square, it's bisected by a center hallway. The bedrooms are on the left as you enter with the master bedroom in front, and two smaller bedrooms behind. Sarah picks the bedroom in the rear. The smallest bedroom in the middle does double duty as a sitting room and guest room, depending on whether the sleeper sofa is unfolded. The living room is in front on the right, and an eat-in kitchen is in the rear. The kitchen has an exit door leading to the driveway. Although architecturally impoverished, the apartment is on one level and is easily negotiated.

Sitting on the floor in the kitchen, I'm startled when my cell phone ringer echoes through the empty rooms. "Hello."

"Ranger Garrison?"

"Speaking."

"This is Pierre Toussant. You have orders to report to me tomorrow morning, yes?"

"Yes, at the Natchitoches office on Route 6."

"I'm looking forward to putting you to work, but I don't want you to sound like a visitor. Try pronouncing the name of the town na'-ku-dish. Have you read the report I sent?"

"I read it."

"We need your help on this one, Ranger."

"That's why I'm here."

"Good, I'll see you tomorrow. Do you need any help getting settled?"

"Not unless you have a truckload of furniture."

"Sorry."

"See you tomorrow then." I look forward to meeting Toussant. My research on the man revealed little. He's been in the service over twenty years. He's unmarried, 44, and lives in a spacious antebellum house in downtown Natchitoches. There's something to be said for the single life. Rangers are moved about at the whim of the service, so it's curious to me that he has stayed at the Kisatchie for most of his career. Perhaps he has a health or family issue that the service considers. I won't ask.

CHAPTER 2

▼

Fortunately, I brought my uniform in the Excursion. Unfortunately, my iron is between moving vans; consequently, I report to Ranger Toussant looking as though I've slept in my clothes. So much for first impressions. Toussant, neat in his pressed uniform, appears six feet tall and 170 pounds. He graciously accepts my story about the absent iron.

"Sit down, Mark," the ranger says, motioning toward a chair next to his small desk. The Natchitoches office of the Ranger District is well lit and economically furnished.

"Thanks, Pierre. Where do we start?"

"Where all law enforcement agents start—with donuts and coffee, and call me Pete." He's found my weak spot. We serve ourselves and return to the desk. Toussant opens a manila folder.

"The report is pretty vague," I say.

"Since I sent the report, we've had more input from the ME."

"What's the cause of death?"

"He's ruled the death a possible homicide. Your first order of business is to get the report and study it, and then take what time you need to get settled in. We'll meet again when you're ready. It's important that we strike while the iron's hot. Think you can get a real iron in the meantime?"

As requested, I pay a call on the ME. I need to know why he's ruled the death a possible homicide. The ME is the only doctor in town, a young man from a Middle Eastern country, probably working off the costs of his subsidized medical education by serving for a specified time in a rural community. His office is in the rear of a community clinic—by appearance, a breeding ground for spewed bacteria. I ask to read his report on the dead girl. "Emil has the report," he says. I assume he's referring to the constable of Roberval.

Emil Lachine is a law enforcement officer in the small Louisiana town of Roberval, located approximately midway between Toussant's office in Natchitoches and the Kisatchie Ranger District, one of several forests in the Kisatchie group. Constable Lachine has the confidence of Pete Toussant and knowledge of the area; as a result, Toussant thinks he'll be an asset in my investigation. Louisiana highway 6 is known historically as the San Antonio Trace. This two-lane road carries traffic from the center of Louisiana at Winnfield to the western border at Toledo Bend Reservoir. There it becomes Texas highway 21, which terminates in San Antonio. The San Antonio Trace and I will become friends. It links my supervisor's office in Natchitoches, the Kisatchie Ranger District, and the home of the constable.

I watch mailboxes until I come to Lachine's place, a manufactured home set off the road the approximate distance of a football field among a stand of scraggly loblolly pines. I drive over a huge storm drainage pipe barely covered by gravel, then follow dirt ruts to where his shiny black town vehicle is parked, a dripping hose coiled nearby. He takes pride in his equipment, a good sign. A hybrid bike is leaning against the trailer—the kind of bike used by a teenager. Lachine's half-acre property is in a natural state, except for a small patch of grass from the driveway to the front door. Stepping out of my SUV, I get the attention of a mongrel that lets me know my presence isn't welcome. Dogs don't scare me, so I take a few steps and offer my hand palm up. He stops barking, studies me for a minute, sniffs my hand, and lies down. As I approach the door I can hear raised voices, so I judiciously postpone knocking. I can barely make out the words.

"You're making me late again, Lettie."

"You wouldn't be late if you'd gotten your sorry butt out of bed on time."

"You still don't have my uniform ready. How many times do I have to tell you that I need a freshly pressed uniform every morning?"

"Don't yell at me. What do you think I'm doin' with this iron, makin' coffee?"

"I'll do more than yell at you if you don't get going."

"Why do you need a freshly-pressed uniform for what you do, Emil? You don't have to have a uniform to sneak up on people to give 'em one of your high-priced tickets. Sittin' and waitin', then stickin' 'em for a couple hundred bucks just for speedin' through this hole-in-the-wall town. If I was one of 'em I couldn't get through this town fast enough. You call that law enforcement? I call that highway robbery and it don't take no genius to do it. With your fancy uniform you oughtta be the sheriff around here getting' the big bucks and rubbin' elbows with the town hotshots."

"You just wait, Lettie. I'm gonna make some big bucks someday. You just wait. Where's Lonnie?"

"He went to school an hour ago. You know, the world doesn't wait for you to get up to get started. Put on your uniform and go to your hidin' place. Give me some peace."

"I'm gonna give you some peace, all right."

"You better get dressed in a hurry. There's a police car in front."

"That ain't a police car. It's one of the rangers from Kisatchie."

I knock and the door opens immediately. A slight man steps onto the porch while buttoning his uniform shirt, and closes the door behind him. His uniform is as neat as his vehicle. I like what I see. He doesn't have a commanding appearance—about five feet eight or so, maybe 145 pounds. His hair is a bit of an Elvis throwback, but his pockmarked, delicately featured face is clean-shaven.

"I'd ask you in, but Lettie isn't expecting company," he says in a soft voice that requires concentrated listening.

"I should have called before coming. I'm sorry." I extend my hand and the constable responds with a firm handshake. "I'm Mark Garrison."

"I thought so. Pete told me you'd need my help. I guess you know who I am. Actually, I was about to go on duty. Do you have a reason for coming?"

"Yes, to introduce myself, and because the ME said that he gave you his report on the Kisatchie victim. I'd like to review it."

"It's in there somewhere," he says, pointing to the door. "I don't have time to find it right now. Suppose I give you a call when I get off duty."

"You mean it's lost?"

"Not really. If you could see the inside of our home, you'd understand. We live sort of casual like."

"I can wait, if you can take a minute to look for it. It's important."

"I'd like to help you, Ranger, but I'm already late. I'll call you." He steps around me and walks to his vehicle without another word, leaving me standing on the porch.

"It's coming today, Sarah. We have to get busy cleaning this place up."

"Let's at least finish our backgammon game, Mom."

"I concede. You've got six pieces off the board and I'm still trying to get my pieces home. You win, okay?"

"That's three in a row."

"Okay, rub it in. All we have is a broom until the truck arrives, so let's sweep the floors."

"We've got to get the stuff I need for school."

"But someone has to be here. The movers are on the way. We'll shop after they leave."

"Mom, are we going to live in this place forever?"

"I know it's not as nice as our house in New Hampshire, honey, but it's a start. We're only renting. We can move when we get to know the area and find a better place, okay? And it's all on one floor, no steps. That's a good thing, right? We'll be a little crowded, but it's a good time to dispose of things we don't need."

"Mom, I really miss Ace," Sarah said, sliding her back along the wall until she was sitting on the floor, her eyes misting.

"I know you do," Lauren replied, sliding down alongside Sarah. "I miss him, too."

"Do you think he'll marry Millie?"

"What makes you think that, Sarah?"

"Just the way he talked about her on the phone."

"She's older than Ace, you know, but they seem to get along well together. Would it be such a bad thing?"

"I guess not. At least they'd each have someone."

"Are you afraid that he'd lose interest in us?"

"Not you. You're his daughter, but maybe me."

"Save your tears, honey. You're closer to Ace than I ever was. I gave him fits, and, besides, he's closer to you. It happens sometimes with grandparents and grandchildren. They often have stronger bonds than parents and their children. Don't ever worry about Ace losing interest in you. Anyway, can't we be happy for them?"

"I guess. Do you think we'll go back to New Hampshire some day?"

"Nothing's impossible, you know, but right now Mark's got a lot of work to do. Once you get settled in school, I'll be helping him, if he'll let me. He's a rare bird in the Forest Service. They don't have many rangers with his experience in law enforcement, plus he'll have help from the locals—the rangers and the local constable."

"Mom, I think I hear the truck out in front."

Pete's on the phone when I return to his office the following morning. He motions for me to come and sit. I pour a cup of coffee, retrieve a donut, and return to my chair as he hangs up.

"Hi, Mark. Ready to work?"

"Stuck in position," I say. "The ME's report is somewhere at Emil's home, and I'm not sure that he knows where."

"Ever been in Emil's house trailer, you'd know the problem. It's usually a disaster. His wife isn't going to win a housekeeping award. The ME dictates his report. Did you ask him whether you could listen to his tapes?"

"That's why you're the supervisor and I'm the guy on the ground, I guess." I start to rise, but Pete motions for me to stay seated.

"This isn't New England, Mark. You'll learn that we do things a bit differently in the south. That's all I'll say. Get your furniture yet?"

"It came yesterday."

"Usable?"

"Pretty much. Some dents and scratches, but it's hard to tell which ones are new. Lauren is getting things settled. She's pretty efficient actually."

"And your girl?"

"She's getting ready to start school."

"You're moving fast, Mark. Why not have a second go at the ME?"

"Thanks, Pete. Later."

"I didn't offer the tapes because you didn't ask for the tapes," the ME tells me. I decide to let the cynicism slide since he's the only doc in town and he might have to dig a bullet out of my chest someday.

"Now I'm asking."

"It's not a problem, Ranger, but Emil returned the written report before you got here. Would you prefer the real thing?" I hadn't asked the right question, I guess.

"Sure." He hands me a copy of the ME's report.

All I'd been told about the incident in Kisatchie was that a naked teenaged girl was found floating face up among cypress knees in a swamp inside the eastern perimeter of the national forest. None of the details were included in my initial letter from Pete, so I read the medical examiner's report carefully. I have already learned from the police report that a man and his wife, after visiting the Longleaf Vista Recreation Area, exited the Kisatchie at the east side onto state highway

119. Unsure about how to enter I-49 from 119, they pulled to the side of the road to check a map. The wife exited the vehicle to take pictures of a cypress swamp known as Bayou Pierre. Using a zoom lens she saw a body lodged between cypress knees approximately 100 feet from the road. They weren't able to receive a signal on their mobile phone, so they returned to the recreation area to report their finding to a forest service volunteer. Louisiana state police and the Natchitoches sheriff's department responded to the volunteer's call, established a crime scene, and posted an officer until the following day when the body was removed by the ME.

The first EMT on the scene declared the time of death at 16:10. After the medical-legal autopsy, the actual time of death was estimated to be at least 2–4 days before the discovery. The ME couldn't be more precise because of the temperature of the water and lengthy immersion of the body. I skim the details of the dissection and internal examination and focus on the externals—no clothing or jewelry was present. The female body weighed 105 pounds and measured sixty-four inches. Either she was a model or undernourished. Her fingerprints were not on record in the parish. The only marks on her body were three piercings of each ear and one piercing of her navel. Two tattoos were evident, one of a six-point star on her right ankle, and one of a rose above her right buttock. The form of a shoe or boot was impressed on her chest across her breasts. Her ribs and sternum were crushed. Fingernails were trimmed and undamaged. There was no evidence of sexual assault. Toxicology tests revealed a high level of alcohol in the girl's blood, sufficient to cause severe intoxication or unconsciousness. Swamp water present in her lungs suggested drowning. The opinion of the ME is that this person died as a result of being held underwater by a foot on her chest until drowned. The state of consciousness of the victim at the time of death could not be determined. The manner of death suggests a homicide.

The report is riddled with notations indicating that photos were taken in support of the narration. One of these photos shows a slight shoe or boot impression on the chest of the victim. I make a mental note to review the photo. Lab tests confirmed that the fluid in the victim's lungs was consistent with the swamp water in which the body was found. The killer stood on the body until the victim drowned, crushing the ribs and sternum. The victim may have been unconscious at the time, which would explain the absence of defensive wounds.

CHAPTER 3

▼

"Millie, why don't you give up this old farm house and come into town to live with me?"

"Ace, you sound like one of those modern men who expect to have a woman without a commitment. What kind of a proposal is that?"

"It isn't a proposal, Millie. It's an invitation. We've been spending time together for almost a year. Isn't it time to shorten the distance between us?"

"Shorten the distance between us? You're a real romantic, Ace."

"Millie, you know we're not kids. I like you and I think you like me."

"I do like you, Ace, but I'm not one of those women who takes up with a man without a commitment."

"What do you mean 'takes up'?"

"What do you mean 'shorten the distance'?"

"Let's stop beating around the bush, Millie. I know we haven't talked about sleeping together, but it's not impossible. We're not dead yet, you know."

"You're a true romantic, Ace, that's for sure. You bowl me over with your subtle talk."

"Okay, I'll put it to you straight. I would like for our friendship to move to the next step."

"Then romance me, Casanova. Maybe we'll get somewhere."

"Okay. Suppose we have dinner in town tonight, and then go to my place for dessert and soft music. Does that sound like a romantic evening?"

"You're on, Romeo. What time?"

"You can't bring that to school, you know," a boy's voice spoke as Sarah placed a canvas backpack into her cart.

"Why not?" she asked, turning toward the voice.

"Because it's not transparent."

"Who carries a transparent backpack?"

"Anyone who wants to get past the front door. It's the latest security thing."

"Security? Is there trouble at the school?"

"Not really, but who knows? Anyway, that's the way it is." Sarah put the canvas pack away and replaced it with an ugly transparent pack. "I'm Lonnie," the boy said, hoping for a response but getting none.

"Do you go to middle school, Lonnie?" Sarah asked.

"Nope."

"High school?"

"Yep, you?"

"Eighth grade, starting tomorrow."

"Just move here?"

"Yes, from New Hampshire."

"Dad a logger?"

"No, a ranger, and he's my stepfather."

"A ranger? Cool. He's not the new guy at Kisatchie, is he?" Sarah's eyes widened.

"He is. How come you know about him?"

"Heard my parents talk about him. He was at our house today. My father's the constable in Roberval."

"I'm Sarah," she said.

"I'm in trouble," Lonnie said, smiling. "I'm keeping my Mom waiting. She's in the car. See you tomorrow."

"Thanks for the help."

"How was your first day at school," I ask as Sarah gets into the Excursion in the school parking lot.

"A disaster."

"Oh?"

"The locker they assigned didn't work. I had to beat on it and it still wouldn't open. Naturally, everyone had to stop and watch. Then they gave me another locker next to the boy's bathroom, and I think every boy on the first floor suddenly had a full bladder.

"Not the best day, huh?"

"I'm not done. Every time I walked into a class everyone looked at me as if my eyes were vertically aligned on my face and then looked down at their desk. I think they all came out of the same womb. I may be the first new kid since this school was built. I didn't hear a friendly voice until I was getting ready to go home."

"At last, a friendly voice. Who was it?"

"Lonnie."

"Lonnie who?"

"You should know."

"Why should I know?"

"You know his dad, the constable."

"No kidding? I suspected he had a teen. I saw a bike in front of his house."

"I met him when I was buying school stuff last night. He saved me from making a fool of myself."

"How so?"

"Long dull story. Anyway, he said that things would get better at school, and he made me think about something."

"What's that?"

"That having a new kid at school was a new experience for the students, too. He's really a nice guy, for a constable's kid." Sarah gives me her elfish grin, which is disarming.

"I'm sure I'll get to meet him. Think you'll be okay here?"

"I'm going to try, Mark." I wondered if I'd ever be "dad".

When we get home the apartment looks lived in. Lauren has unpacked the essentials. While Sarah recaps the trials of her day for her mom I go out in search of a bottle of wine. When I find a drive-in liquor store across from a crawfish restaurant I know I'm in Louisiana. At home the satellite radio is playing elevator music and Sarah's arranging her bedroom. I take Lauren by the hand and lead her to the love seat, the only piece of furniture that isn't under a stack of cartons.

"Did you get the ME's report?" she asks.

"Music playing and no teen underfoot, and you ask about the ME's report. Where's your sense of romance?"

"I've got a cluttered house and an anxious daughter, and I'm over a thousand miles from home. You want romance?"

"Guess my timing is off."

"Come here, you goof. I'll show you romance." She moves over to my lap, puts her arms around my neck and kisses me like a teenager in the back seat. I'm hoping that Sarah will stay in her room.

"You know, we haven't been by ourselves since we left New Hampshire."

"Tonight we'll be in our bedroom on a real mattress." I slip my hand under Lauren's blouse and caress her breast. "Later, Ranger."

At four o'clock, I drive through the Kisatchie to Bayou Pierre. The five districts of the Kisatchie National Forest are located in the center of Louisiana. The Kisatchie Ranger District, where the victims were found, is south of Natchitoches. From LA 119 I can see strips of yellow crime scene tape still hanging from a cluster of bald cypress trees about thirty yards from the road. I'm not prepared for swamp wading so I make my observations from dry ground. The descending sun to the west casts eerie reflections on the swamp making the cypress trees look taller than their customary hundred feet. Although cypress trees aren't unknown on the East Coast, these are ancient trees that, at eye level, resemble the legs of giant elephants standing in shallow swamp water. Their roots are widespread and shallow with "knees" sticking out of the water to "breathe" the oxygen above. Moss covers much of the trunks and the branches are budding with tiny needles and the beginning of tiny cones. Standing silently in the midst of this venerable, gray forest one can hear the sounds of swamp life preparing for its night activities. Movements in the water suggest reptilian action, but the only sounds are from frogs and birds, at least to this native Midwesterner's ears.

My imagination is kicked into high gear and I step a little further away from the water. I can't even imagine someone carrying the body of an unconscious young woman thirty yards into the swamp, then standing on her chest until her lungs filled with the dark bayou water. I'm on the hunt for a real swine.

I return home by way of the Longleaf Trail Scenic Byway, a seventeen-mile ride through the heart of the district. The byway skirts a one-and-one-half mile interpretive trail from which a hiker can see the Kisatchie Hills Wilderness Area from naturally carved overlooks. I walk the trail and familiarize myself with native plants and wildlife. Southern magnolias, the state flower, are in bloom, along with dogwoods. Loblolly and longleaf pine trees make up the bulk of the forest and are a major commercial crop in Louisiana. They stand over 100 feet tall and compete at the tops for sunlight. Unlike northern forests, hardwood is less evident. I make a mental note to bring Lauren and Sarah to the Longleaf Vista Trail when the plants are in full bloom.

There is little traffic on the roads and trails in the Kisatchie. The crime could have been committed in broad daylight.

"You're home at last," Lauren says as I walk into the side door leading into the kitchen.

"Where's Sarah?" I ask.

"At her first ballet class."

"Then we're alone?"

"Yes, do you have a reason for asking?"

"I left something unfinished." I walk to the cabinet, lift Lauren off her step-stool and carry her into the master bedroom. She's as light as a feather in my arms. Her long dark hair spills over my shoulder. She could pass for a college cheerleader.

"What are you doing?" she asks in an inviting voice. I put her down on the edge of the bed.

"Your timing isn't exactly great. Look at me. I've been doing hard labor since you left this afternoon, and I feel like a mess."

"I need to have some time alone with you, Lauren. After all, we're still on our honeymoon."

"If you have something in mind, you'll have to let me shower."

"That sounds like a great place to start. Is the shower big enough for two?"

CHAPTER 4

▼

I pick Sarah up at her ballet lesson while Lauren sets the table for dinner. We drive home in silence. Sarah doesn't respond to any of my conversation starters. I write it off to adjustment overload. She passes her mother in the kitchen without a word and goes directly to her room. Lauren looks at me as I come into the kitchen.

"Where's our little girl?" I ask.

"In her room—she didn't say a word when she came in. Just went straight to her room."

"She didn't talk on the way home, either. What's up?"

"I don't know. Tell her that dinner's ready. Let's see what happens."

I tap on her door—nothing. I tap harder—still nothing. I return to the kitchen. "She doesn't answer when I knock on her door." Lauren goes to Sarah's door and enters. From through her door, I can see Sarah on her bed staring up at the ceiling.

"Did I interrupt something?" Lauren asks.

"No."

"It's time for dinner."

"Okay." We all go to the table, but again Sarah says nothing until she asks to be excused.

"Is there anything you want to talk about?" Lauren asks.

"No. I'd just like to be left alone." She leaves the table, closes her door, and isn't seen again until morning.

"What do we know about the victim?" I ask Pete.

"Very little."

"Any reports of a missing girl?"

"Nope, and her prints didn't match anything we have. No evidence of dental work done."

"Where does the investigation stand?"

"We've been waiting for you, Ranger." I have a hard time with this kind of crime fighting.

"I'll check the surrounding parishes for missing person reports. The ME's pictures are not very helpful. Her face was badly bloated and distorted—in the putrefaction stage."

"I'll be anxious to hear what you learn."

I hit pay dirt when I contact the Caddo Parish sheriff's office. A young woman matching the description of our victim disappeared eight months previously from Shreveport, following the armed robbery of a liquor store. Apparently, she was driving the getaway car for a young man who was shot and killed during the robbery. The girl's name is Beth Beckett.

On my way to the Caddo Parish sheriff's office in Shreveport my cell phone rings. It's Lauren. She sounds upset. "Sarah's principal called. They want us to come to the school right away. Something's up, but they won't discuss it with me. Where are you?"

"On my way to Shreveport, but I'll turn around. I can probably pick you up in forty-five minutes."

"Thanks." I hang up and call the sheriff's office to reschedule my appointment.

"Not necessary for you to come up," the missing person's clerk responds. "I'll send whatever I have on Ms. Beckett to the Ranger's office. Call again if we need to talk." I reverse direction at the first cloverleaf and head for home. Lauren is sitting on a picnic bench outside the apartment and rushes to the SUV as I turn into the driveway.

"Any new information?" I ask.

"They called again and said to go to the hospital. Apparently, Sarah is there, but they wouldn't say why." In less than ten minutes we're standing in front of the admissions desk, our pulses racing. "We're Sarah Adams' parents. We're told that she's been brought here from the middle school."

"She's in intensive care," the clerk says. "You'll have to wait here for a minute." She disappears behind double doors.

"Wait, please." Lauren says, but she's talking to closed doors. In a matter of seconds two people step out with the admissions clerk—the middle school principal and a parish police officer.

"You can't see your daughter right now," the admissions clerk says. "She's being treated, but these gentlemen can tell you what happened." She leads us into the family counseling room.

After introductions, the principal says, "Hello, Mr. and Mrs. Garrison. Sarah collapsed at her locker this morning. We called for help, not knowing what her condition was, and they brought her here. They tell us that she is in an alcoholic coma. Does Sarah have a drinking problem?" Lauren looks stunned.

"Of course not! What are you talking about?"

"Please. I'm just telling you what we've been told. The doctors are working very hard with Sarah. I'll see if I can get a medical person to join us." The principal leaves and our attention turns to the police officer.

"Why are you here?" I ask.

"I accompanied the ambulance. Whenever we have a minor involved in an alcohol incident, it's a police matter, Mr. Garrison."

"How so?"

"We'll want to know who provided the alcohol to Sarah, and we'll have to consider bringing charges against Sarah when she recovers." I speak before Lauren can remove the officer's head.

"This is out of character for Sarah. I'm not aware that she has ever had a drink of liquor."

"Alcoholics are very good at hiding their problem, especially from parents." This was all Lauren could take.

"Listen, I know you're doing your job. We're all law enforcement people here, but if you think I'm going to stand for Sarah being charged with anything, think again. She has never had a drink, period, before this."

"Ma'am, it's not a matter of choice. Whether a charge is made will be determined by the facts, but I can tell you that this is not the first time we've had alcohol problems at the school and we're taking it pretty seriously."

"Excuse me," a nurse interrupts. "Are you the Adams family?"

"No, we're the Garrison family, but Sarah Adams is our daughter. Can we see her now?" Lauren asks.

"I'm sorry. As soon as she's conscious, we'll bring you in. She has a high blood alcohol content and we have to clean out her system. It's difficult to predict the outcome. We'll keep you informed." She reaches toward Lauren and takes her hand. "Is there any way that we can make you more comfortable?"

"No, thank you," Lauren replies, surrendering her stoic posture. The officer understands my hand motion and leaves the family counseling room with the nurse. I have no words of consolation. I hold Lauren tightly and let her cry it out.

Lauren doesn't have a faith system. Ace did a tremendous job raising Lauren and caring for Sarah, but the one thing that's missing in their lives is a faith system—trusting in someone besides themselves when things get tough. As I walk to the hospital cafeteria to get coffee for what's going to be a long night, I wonder whether she'd be open to praying for Sarah. I'm sure she would be, but we've never discussed it. She attended church with me once in New Hampshire, but she did it to please me, so I haven't pushed it. Judy and I had grown in faith together and had made God a partner in our marriage.

I ask Lauren if she'd like to pray. "Here?" she asks.

"Why not?"

"We're not alone, in case you haven't noticed."

"We can go to the chapel. It's on the way to the cafeteria and there's no one there. I looked."

"I suppose it can't hurt." Her response is accommodating at best. We sip our coffee and wait for word from the ICU.

At eleven thirty, as Lauren paces the hallway and I sit in the ICU waiting lounge, a man in green scrubs approaches. "Mr. and Mrs. Garrison?"

"Yes."

"I'm Dr. Ward. May I speak with you for a moment?"

"Are you taking care of Sarah?"

"I'm part of Sarah's team."

"How's she doing?"

"We'll know more in another twenty-four hours, but she's hanging on. We have her heart rate and breathing at normal levels, but she hasn't regained consciousness."

"What do you do in cases like this?" I ask.

"You mean cases of alcohol poisoning? We're trying to counter the effects of alcohol on her system. A complicated metabolic process within the body turns the alcohol into a dangerous acid called formic acid. We're administering sodium bicarbonate intravenously to counter the acid, and we're using a relatively new drug to keep the acid from forming. At the same time we have her on hemodialysis to help eliminate the harmful chemicals. We're also helping her maintain a good blood pressure and breathing rate since alcohol depresses these functions.

This is about all that we can do at present. We'll know more when she regains consciousness, which could be soon."

"Will she …" Lauren can't finish the sentence.

"Get better?" the doctor offers. "Probably. The only unknown right now is whether there will be permanent damage."

"Permanent how?"

"To her brain."

"Is that likely?" I ask.

"We just don't know."

"What kind of alcohol did she take, and how much?" Lauren asks.

"We don't know how much. It doesn't take much for a person unused to drinking to be poisoned, and if she drank the alcohol in a short period of time, it's more complicated. Binge drinkers can drink lethal amounts of alcohol before they pass out. You see, the damage continues long after they're unconscious because of the residual alcohol in their stomach and intestines. By the slight smell, I would say that she drank something like vodka. It's undetectable in a non-drinking environment like a school because it's almost odorless. I'd also guess that she drank a lot in a short period of time. Do you have any other questions?"

"Will you let us know when she wakes up?" Lauren asks.

"Of course. I'll be on call when she regains consciousness, but just so that you aren't alarmed, she won't look very good. She'll be confused even without brain damage and she'll be very pale, almost bluish. If you've ever had too much to drink, you know that you don't come to your senses very quickly. My suggestion to you is that you go home, get some sleep, and come back late tomorrow morning. We'll call if anything happens before then. This way, Sarah's head will be clearer and she may be able to answer your questions. My guess right now is that she's going to recover completely, but it wouldn't hurt for you to do a little praying." At this, he left the room. I take Lauren by the hand and lead her to the chapel. She doesn't object.

Neither of us sleeps. We try, but after an hour or so of respectful silence, Lauren switches on the light and rolls over to face me. "Coffee?" I ask.

"Yes."

"Want to talk?"

"Yes." While I'm making coffee, Lauren comes into the kitchen in her bathrobe and sits at the kitchen table. She isn't wearing anything under her robe and I try to conceal my untimely attraction to her. "How did we miss this?"

"I'm not sure."

"Last night she was so quiet. I should have done something."

"Lauren, if you're going to blame yourself for what happened, you'll become part of the problem instead of part of the solution. Please, let's stay on point here and focus on what we do next, okay?"

"I hate your logic, but I know you're right. Okay, Mark, where do we go from here?"

At nine o'clock the phone rings. "Mr. Garrison, your daughter is awake and asking for you." I thank the nurse for what I hope is good news and we hurry to the hospital. When we arrive, Sarah's nurse informs us that Sarah is still shaky and has experienced some seizures after waking.

"It's a good thing she was at school when this happened. We got her just in time," the nurse adds.

"I don't understand," Lauren replies.

"If she'd been alone, there's no telling what might have happened. We got her cleaned out just in time. Please follow me." She leads us up one floor to a private room. Sarah is lying on her side facing a window looking over a courtyard. Lauren goes ahead of me and rushes to her daughter.

"Hi," she says cautiously, taking Sarah's shaky hand. Sarah turns to face her mother. She looks awful—pale, eyes bloodshot, hands and chin trembling. Her heart and head are wired to monitors.

"Hi, Mom. I'm really sorry."

"Is it uncomfortable to talk?"

"No, but could we talk alone?" I make an excuse to go to the bathroom and Lauren gives me a smile of thanks.

Since we hadn't had breakfast before the nurse's call, I'm hungry. Hospital cafeteria food is not my first choice usually, but the scrambled eggs and sausages are pretty good. I glance at the morning paper, have a second cup of coffee, call Pete, and then after what I think is the right amount of time, return to Sarah's room. Lauren is in a chair by the bed. Sarah sleeps while the nurse adjusts her monitors. I tap lightly on the door and motion for Lauren to join me in the hall. "What next?" I ask.

"Next we go home." On the way Lauren downloads some of what Sarah has shared. Towards the end of Sarah's first week in school she felt totally isolated. Only Lonnie had spoken to her and only twice. The previous day two girls and a boy approached her at her locker and struck up a conversation. They seemed nice enough. They asked whether she liked the school. When Sarah said that the school was okay, but the kids were cold, they offered to be her friends, if she was cool. Cool meant joining their little group. Joining their little group meant drinking with them.

"I don't drink alcohol," Sarah told them. They told her that she'd probably get along great with the other nerds and started to leave. Eventually, they convinced her to take a sip from one of the girls' insulated mugs. With their urging, she drank the entire contents and doesn't remember anything after that.

"It's a tough age, Lauren. Teens need peer support. When they can't get it where they want it, they take what they can get. Kids her age are also prone to taking risks, thinking they're invincible, and the level of the risks they're willing to take is in proportion to the support they get at home. Sarah has had good support, Lauren. Don't misunderstand what I'm going to say, but she's made some significant changes in the past months—a step dad, a move, separation from Ace and her boy friend, a stay-at-home Mom, and shared attention. I'd be surprised if she hadn't responded to the first offer of friendship at school.

"There's something else, Mark," Lauren interrupts. "Her bio-dad was, and may still be, an alcoholic."

This is the first time Lauren's spoken of Sarah's biological father. We have a standing agreement about that—don't ask, don't tell, and that includes Sarah. "Why do you tell me this now?"

"Because the tendency toward alcoholism is inherited. I'm not an alcoholic, Mark, but her bio-dad, as Sarah likes to refer to him, was an alcoholic when I last saw him."

"Be that as it may, it certainly doesn't mean that Sarah ..."

"I know what you're going to say, and you may be right, but once an alcoholic begins drinking, the fuse has been lit."

"Are you going to tell Sarah about her bio-dad?"

"I haven't told either of you about him, Mark, and maybe it's time that I did. It certainly can do him no harm now. He was my commanding officer in the Army. I thought we were in love, but as soon as I mentioned marriage he broke it off. Having a relationship with an enlisted person was against the rules and he was already on notice because of his drinking. His career was more important than we were. I don't know if he ever learned about Sarah. I never heard from him after the breakup, and I resigned the service when I learned that I was pregnant. Dad wanted me to push for support from him, but I had no interest in that. Now you know, Mark, and I'll tell Sarah when I'm ready, okay? In the meantime, it's between us. I only mention it because I've had to deal with this issue of alcohol before."

CHAPTER 5

▼

I drop Lauren off at the apartment and head for Sarah's school. I want to know who lit Sarah's fuse.

"We don't know who provided the liquor for Sarah, but the police will be following up on this. We're hoping she didn't bring it from home." The principal can see that I'm riled and regrets his remark. "I'm not accusing you, Mr. Garrison, you understand."

"It's Ranger Garrison, and she didn't get her liquor at home. As far as we know, Sarah has never had a drink of liquor before this. Her mother and I have an occasional drink of wine. She got it here."

"If that's so, we'll find the source. This isn't the first liquor incident we've had in the past year, and the sheriff is getting some pressure from our parents."

"Do you mind if I do a little snooping around?"

"Not as long as you keep the administration and sheriff's office informed."

"Who called the ambulance for Sarah?"

"The school secretary. A student saw Sarah congregating at her locker with some other students, and then saw her pass out. The student went to the office."

"Did she see who was with Sarah?"

"You'll have to ask her. I can arrange to have her come to the office."

I wait in the office for about half an hour for the student to arrive. Finally, the principal returns and tells me that the student has been absent since Sarah's incident. Contact at home has been unsuccessful. The school will release her personal information only to the sheriff's office.

I start to dial the sheriff's office, then decide I should talk with Pete first.

Pete's in a conference when I walk into his office, presumably with Constable Lachine, whose Roberval vehicle is parked outside. When the conference ends, Lachine glances briefly at me on his way out of the building. Pete motions me to join him. "What did you say to the principal?" he asks. "Have you been conducting an investigation at the school?"

"I asked a few questions about Sarah's situation, yes."

"Lachine is a little sensitive about rangers probing into civilian matters. He advised the principal to deal directly with him on police issues."

"I thought his jurisdiction is Roberval. The school isn't in Roberval."

"It doesn't really matter, Mark. Law enforcement agencies cooperate. The police juries and parish sheriffs work together. As federal law enforcement officers we're out of their loop."

"What the heck is a police jury? I feel as though I'm in a foreign country."

"In a sense you are. Let me give you a history lesson." Pete pours two cups of coffee, puts one in front of me, leans back, and swings his feet to the top of his desk. "Louisiana's form of government is influenced by the old Napoleonic Code. Louisiana was first formed into 12 counties. In 1807 it was divided into 19 parishes based on the church parishes. Today there are 64 parishes and the designation 'county' has been dropped entirely. Judges once governed the parishes, but today the citizens elect a 'police jury' comprised of jurors, the number depending on the population of the parish. The juries have general authority, much like a county commission where you're from. Consider other states where cities, townships, and counties all cooperate to achieve local law enforcement and provide services. It works that way here, too, Mark, except that we call them by different names. You'll get used to it."

"How come you're so well informed about local politics?"

"Do you know how many visitors to the forest ask the same question? Your comment was close to the truth. Living in Louisiana is like living in another country. It has a history all its own."

"So, Constable Lachine has charge of an investigation outside of Roberval? Why not the parish sheriff?"

"They're working together, I assume. What matters, Mark, is that we have no authority there."

"Then am I supposed to let the matter involving Sarah drop?"

"I've asked Lachine to keep you wired in. Talk to him, Mark. You're going to need his help in the Kisatchie matter. Stay on his good side. I'll stay in tune with the sheriff. We're fellow Rotarians."

"Do you know which student reported Sarah's matter to the principal?"

"No, but if it's important, I'll find out. You might also ask Lachine." I leave the office and drive the San Antonio Trace toward Roberval.

On the way, I fall into a perfect speed trap. As I enter Roberval in my Excursion I see a reduced speed sign and begin slowing to forty-five. Within minutes a blinding light and siren come up behind me. Recognizing Lachine's town vehicle, I pull to the shoulder. After a few minutes he approaches my window. "Well, Ranger, we're in a hurry, aren't we?"

"Hello, Constable. Actually, I was hoping to see you, but not like this."

"It's how I greet speeders."

"I'm certain that I slowed to the legal speed when I saw the sign."

"That's a bit of a problem. You see, you should have been at the legal speed when you passed the second sign."

"There were two signs? I must have missed the first."

"Apparently so. Next time you'll know." He puts his ticket book back in his pocket. "What do you want to see me about?"

"The incident at my daughter's school."

"I understand you were there asking questions."

"As a father."

"That's not the impression you gave the principal. He was surprised that the Forest Service was making inquiries."

"I've already been reminded about territorial protocol, Constable, but I intend to get to the bottom of the matter as Sarah's father. I'm sure you can understand that. Do you know which student observed her collapse?"

"I've checked around. If I find out, I'll let you know."

"I'd appreciate that. Thank you. Am I free to go?"

"Slowly."

I turn around. After several miles I make a U-turn and return in the direction of Roberval. The constable's right. There are two speed limit signs; however, the first sign is almost entirely obscured by an overgrown shrub. It's clearly a money-making shrub. It's unlikely that any driver could slow to legal speed before reaching the second sign. Pete laughs when I tell him about my Roberval experience. It's a local joke.

On the following morning I ask Lauren, "What time are you going to pick up Sarah?"

"She'll be released at ten, after a conference with the doctor."

"I'll be home when you get back. Pete called with the name of the girl that reported Sarah's situation to the principal. I'll be driving to her home this morning."

The witness at Sarah's school is Cindy Malvineaux. Pete doesn't have her address, but I find two Malvineaux's in the Natchitoches phone book. I opt for the one closest to home and hit pay dirt, in a way. The family lives in a fashionable house in town. A thirty-something woman opens the door. After identifying myself, she invites me to step in, but doesn't move far from the door. "May I speak to your daughter?"

"She's sleeping right now. It's not a good time."

"It's a school day. Shouldn't she be in school?" As we talk I see a young woman walk across the hallway at the top of the stairs. She turns briefly and looks my way. The skin around her eyes is yellow—the color of black eyes healing.

"I guess you can see why she's not in school."

"What happened?"

"I'd really rather not talk about it." She moves toward the door and stands, waiting for me to leave.

"I need to know what she saw, who was with my daughter when she collapsed."

"She won't be able to tell you. She can't remember."

"But it was less than a week ago."

"She can't remember. I'm sorry. I've got to go to her now. You'll have to leave."

Lauren has Sarah home when I return. They're in the living room. "How are you feeling?" I ask.

"I'm okay, I guess. I'm really hungry, Mom."

"I'll fix lunch for all of us." Lauren says, stepping into the kitchen.

"Sarah, I need to know what happened at school. Try to remember who gave you the liquor."

"Why, Mark? So you can get me into trouble?" I'm stunned by her response. "No one forced me to drink it. I didn't know I'd get so sick. It was a dare by some kids who wanted to be my friends. Life here isn't exactly a social whirlwind, you know."

"Those aren't the kind of friends you need, Sarah. You could have died."

"Maybe that would have been an improvement, Mark. I'm really hungry and tired. Could we end the interrogation?"

"Sarah, your Mom and I love you and want you to be safe, but I'm not sure how to make that happen."

Sarah gets up and heads for her bedroom. Over her shoulder she says, "If you really want that, Mark, take me home." She closes her door.

"Did you hear that?" I ask Lauren as she returns to the living room.

"I heard."

"What's going on? In the hospital she was remorseful."

"Now she's angry, Mark. I don't really think she knows what she feels."

"You know I can't leave now, Lauren, but you can. Do you want to take her back to New Hampshire?"

"I think we should consider that after your work here is done."

"I wasn't sent here on a temporary assignment. I was transferred here, Lauren."

"Let's keep our options open, Mark, okay? I'll work with Sarah. You finish your investigation. And, by the way, Mark, there's something else." She hands me an envelope. "What's this?" I ask, taking the envelope.

"Read it," Lauren replies. I open the envelope and read a letter from Ace to Lauren.

"Dear Lauren,

Hi sweetheart. Well, it's happened. Your old man is going to get married again. Millie and I have decided to tie the knot this spring, maybe next month. The date is open for now. How's that for a couple of old fogies? We've both decided that we get along, hate to live alone, enjoy life, and want to enjoy it together. Now, don't think that there's no romance in this relationship—there's plenty! We're even holding hands! We decided that before this gets to home base, we'd better do the right thing. I hope you'll be pleased. Oh, sure, you can think of a few reasons why this doesn't make sense, but we won't get too many more chances for happiness in our old age, so we're going to do it. Now, we don't want to be running off and eloping, so here's what we thought. We want Pastor Kraft to do the wedding here in Woodsville, then we could come to Louisiana for our honeymoon, maybe even see New Orleans on the way there or back. What do you think? I didn't call because I didn't want to hear the tone of your voices. Take a minute, think it over, and give us a call, okay? We both love you all. Give a special hug to my sweetie, Sarah.

Love, Dad"

I'm not sure what to say. "Has Sarah read this?"

"Not yet. It's not the right time. Let's keep it to ourselves for awhile. I think it would be good to go back for the wedding and have a vacation for a week or so, after school is out."

"I agree. I'll see if I can make some real progress on the investigation and find some slack time to relax. Why not write to Ace and tell him that May or June would work out best for us."

"I'll call Dad. I need to talk to him. He doesn't know about Sarah's situation and I'm not going to tell him. They're on cloud nine right now."

"I'm going to review the ME's report again. Will you be okay if I leave?"

"I'll be okay. Sarah wants to return to school tomorrow, so I'm going to have to get some things ready. We have to meet with the principal before she can be readmitted."

I need time to gather my thoughts, so I drive to the Kisatchie and hike in the Longleaf Vista Recreation Area. The investigation doesn't feel like a team effort. I'm bumping into too many walls—the ME, Lachine, and even Pete's lackadaisical approach. There isn't much enthusiasm for solving the homicide. And then there's Sarah and her attitude, the jurisdictional matter, the memory-impaired witness, and the alcohol. What did the principal mean when he referred to "other problems with alcohol?" And, finally, the two homicides in the cypress swamp. The first, a year earlier, is now a cold case, but this latest one is on my plate. Where to turn? The ME's report—I should look at the photos.

I sit down on a log and watch a Louisiana milk snake crawl lazily across the toe of my boot, then disappear among some leaves. Its magnificent red and black colorings remind me that I am where I most want to be—in the woods. It brings to mind the years I spent on the Appalachian Trail working with Dave Kraft. Those were good times. Like Sarah, I miss New Hampshire. I force myself to return to my vehicle and to the ME's file.

On the way back to Natchitoches I stop at the community clinic and review the autopsy photos, especially the photo of Ms. Beckett's chest. The report noted that a shoe print was seen across the breast line. It isn't apparent to me in the photo, but clearly there are abrasions on her chest that take the shape of a shoe or boot. Her skin is badly mottled and deteriorated, perhaps from insect infestation. The boot or shoe abrasions, approximately twelve inches in length, are in line with the woman's breasts. Her chest is flattened, thus the broken ribs and sternum. Since the swamp is no more than knee deep the killer must have forced Ms. Beckett to the bottom by standing on her chest. If she was unconscious, it took no effort to keep her under water until she drowned. The ME noted that she was probably in an alcoholic coma.

My mind goes into a swirl—alcohol seems to be a key issue in my investigation, and my life—Ms. Beckett, Sarah, the school, Lauren's first husband, my own mother. Is there a message here? Does alcohol play into this girl's death as it almost had with Sarah? If not for alcohol, could Ms. Beckett have fought back? Would she be alive and on the run today? Is alcohol a coincidental common denominator or a pervasive problem in general?

I ask Pete to send a print of the "boot" photo and the report to the FBI lab for advice. I want to know whether it's possible to identify the footwear and weight of the bearer. I'm out on a limb and know it, but amazing things happen in crime labs these days. "It'll be awhile before these results, if any, will be available," Pete reminds me.

On the following morning I visit the Caddo Parish sheriff in Shreveport. "What do you know about Ms. Beth Beckett?" I ask the distinguished looking black lawman.

"Not much. We know that she assisted in a liquor store robbery and then left the area."

"Did she have a criminal record?"

"Minor stuff—truancy as a youngster, some shoplifting episodes, and recurring runaways."

"I'd like to visit her parents. Do you have a home address?" He copies an address, but can't be sure it's current. I drive through a squalid neighborhood to a house that's been converted to four apartments according to the mailbox. A narrow sidewalk leads me through uncollected trash to the rear of the building. I climb to the second level of an enclosed porch and knock. Through the door I can see a sparsely furnished, messy apartment. Beer cans litter a Formica kitchen table, and the refrigerator door is standing slightly ajar. A forty-something woman comes to the door holding her unbuttoned housecoat together. I introduce myself and she backs away from the door, and then collapses into a kitchen chair. I follow her into the kitchen.

"What kind of cop are you?" she slurs, looking at my ranger uniform.

"I'm a Forest Service ranger."

"Well, you came to the right forest." She lets her housecoat fall open to expose herself.

"Please cover yourself, Ma'am. I'd like to ask a few questions about your daughter, Beth."

"What about her? She in trouble again?"

"You haven't heard from her recently?"

"Get on with it, forest cop. I got stuff to do."

"Ma'am, I'm sorry to tell you that your daughter is dead." I let it sit there. She sits up a little straighter. No tears, no stares, no questions—just a momentary reposturing. I let myself out.

CHAPTER 6

▼

That afternoon Pete attended a meeting of the Rotary Club and returned with some news. "The sheriff leaned on Cindy Malvineaux's mother and got the name of one of the boys who was in the group that gave alcohol to Sarah."

"Thanks, Pete. Is he going to follow up?"

"He already has, but there's nothing to report. The boy didn't actually handle the liquor. He was with the group, but he wouldn't name his companions. This is a tight group apparently. It's the first lead the sheriff has had on a series of alcohol related incidents, including possession by minors, public intoxication, assault while under the influence, driving with open containers, and so on. The kids clam up when they're questioned about where they're getting the booze. He has an undercover female trying to buy from parish liquor stores without an id, but with no success. The storeowners aren't part of the problem. The kids seem to have an underground source. One of these days someone is going to die."

"Someone almost did."

"I know, Mark."

"What can I do, Pete?"

"Keep looking for the source of the liquor. That'll answer several questions."

"It's good to see you back in school, Sarah, How are you feeling?"

"Better than last week, Lonnie. Does everyone know what happened?"

"Are you kidding? In this school? If you drop your pencil, it's headline news."

"What are they saying?"

"Not much. There's something going on, but I don't know what it is."

"Something going on?"

"Yeah, the losers are scared, backing off, cutting classes. No one wants to get blamed, I guess. I think they're afraid that you're going to turn them in. Are you?"

"Nobody's asked me except my stepfather. Nobody forced me to drink, Lonnie. I don't blame anyone but myself."

"Did you tell your Dad?"

"Step dad."

"Sorry."

"It's okay. He's okay, too, I guess. He's good to my Mom. It's just being here that sucks."

"Thanks."

"I just miss New Hampshire and I'd like to go back."

"Don't look now, but here comes one of your so-called friends. Want me to stay?"

"For what? I can take care of myself. It's better if you don't get involved."

"Later."

"Hey, Sarah."

"Hey."

"Listen, I'm sorry about what happened. We didn't mean for you to get sick."

"You didn't force me. What do you want?"

"Just to tell you I'm sorry."

"Okay, you're sorry. Now I've got to get to class."

"The others want to know whether you told anyone about us."

"Why?"

"Why? Because we'd be in a lot of trouble, that's why? It would be best if you didn't, you know?"

"Is that a threat?"

"Take it anyway you want, Sarah. We want to be your friends, not your enemies."

"Friends don't do what you did."

"Sarah, listen to me. Nothing will happen to you if you let it go, understand?"

"That sounds like another threat."

"Goodbye, Sarah."

My investigation of the Kisatchie drowning is fast becoming another cold case. The FBI has no way to determine the weight or size of the killer from the picture of the impression on the body. The tread mark on Ms. Beckett's chest was deep and wide, common to hiking shoes or boots. The size of the footwear is between ten and one-half and twelve and the width is narrow. The tread pattern is too uncertain to determine the make.

I'm losing my enthusiasm for the case when I report to Pete. "Neither Constable Lachine or I have come up with anything substantial in the case." Pete senses my frustration.

"I've got a great idea. You need a rest. There's a service boat on a trailer in the alley behind the office. It's got a small motor. Why don't you take it to Toledo Bend Reservoir and do some bass fishing. They're biting right now. Do you like to fish?"

"I thought you'd never ask. Lauren might like to join me. She likes outdoor sports. Thanks, Pete."

"Be sure to tell Lachine that you're going to take a few days off, just in case."

"Just in case of what? He hasn't been much help, to be honest."

"Do me the favor, please."

Lauren is excited. We decide to go fishing on Friday evening and Saturday morning. When I ask Sarah whether she wants to go, she wrinkles her nose and shakes her head. I call Emil, move the boat to our driveway, and buy tackle at the discount store.

On Friday evening, we launch the boat at a ramp on the Louisiana side of the Toledo Bend Bridge and then put-put our way through the stumps to where several fishing boats are anchored. It isn't long before we have our limit of crappie and bass. Lauren doesn't clean fish, but she's eager to fry them. Even Sarah enjoys the feast.

On Saturday morning we get up early and return to the same launch ramp. Shortly after launching, I notice water in the bottom of the boat. I assume that we drew water when we put the boat in, but when we reach our fishing spot the water seems deeper. With my bait bucket I begin to bail while Lauren checks to make sure we inserted the drain plug. It's in place. How is the water getting in? We had rowed to position so as not to disturb the fish, but we decide to motor back and find the source of the leak. The motor sputters for a minute and then dies. I try everything I can think of to get the motor running before the boat sinks. Finally, I check the gas tank. It's empty. How can this be? I filled it on Friday. I notice three small holes in the bottom of the boat where the can was sitting. It isn't unusual to have bottom leaks with so many stick-ups, but these holes are all the same size, round, and by the way the metal is bent, I can tell that they've been drilled. With the fuel can removed, the water comes in faster. "Lauren, you bail while I row us back. We're in trouble."

The water in the boat is six to eight inches deep when we limp to the dock. If we had rowed farther out, the boat would have swamped and we would have been in deep trouble. Swimming in Toledo Bend Reservoir is impossible with the stumps and undergrowth, not to mention the alligators. If I had been alone, unable to bail and row, I would have been sunk. "Someone has drilled holes in the boat and emptied our fuel tank."

"Who would do that, Mark?"

"I don't know, but I intend to find out."

"When could they have done it?"

"Sometime during the night in our driveway."

"Who knew that we were going fishing besides Pete, Sarah, and Emil?"

I tell Pete what happened, but he blows it off. "Toledo Bend is notorious for puncturing holes in boats. The stick-ups are especially bad when the water level is low, like it is now. Most fishermen have their boat bottoms reinforced with a gorilla hull. Did that old gas can leak? I'll have it replaced, Mark. Sorry you had so much trouble out there. Fishing Toledo Bend takes some practice. You'll get used to it."

"We had no problems on Friday. What happened on Saturday was not from inexperience or bad equipment. Someone deliberately tried to put us in danger."

"Why, and who?" he asks. He dismisses the idea and implies that I'm an amateur fisherman. He even offers to go out with me on my next fishing adventure. That'll be a cold day in hell.

I retrieve and refill the gas can—it doesn't leak. The holes in the bottom of the boat are not punched through from the bottom; they are drilled through from the top. I don't need a crime lab to tell me that what happened was deliberate. Whoever did it hadn't expected me to survive or the boat to float or they would have been more careful. I'm a threat to someone.

Ballet proves good for Sarah's spirit. A superior and likable student, she's successful at making friends. One of the boys in her class, the son of a Lutheran minister, gets her involved in youth activities at his father's church. Little by little, she puts the alcohol event behind her.

As her attitude improves, she also becomes more open with me. I don't push her to tell me who was involved in the school matter, but on a drive to school she volunteers the information. She reveals the names of the three who approached her and offered her the alcohol. She confirms that the boy whose name I already know was more of an observer than a participant. The other boy and girl were the pushers. In the interest of jurisdictional protocol, I share this information with Emil.

As Sarah adjusts to her new life, Lauren is getting bored. Having been a law enforcement officer most of her adult life, she's bored in the role of homemaker, especially in our small apartment. Raised by Ace, trained in outdoor sports and military service, Lauren is more comfortable in a man's world. Ladies groups simply aren't enterprising enough. I can sense her discontent. "How would you like to help me, unofficially of course, in my investigation?"

"How?"

"I'm not sure, but Pete and Emil aren't self-starters and I'm running out of time. It's been over two weeks since we left New Hampshire and I'm not getting anywhere on the Kisatchie investigation."

"I might be able to help while Sarah's in school, Mark. What exactly do you have in mind?"

"I can't follow up on Sarah's alcohol issue; Pete and Emil have me in a straight jacket, but there's nothing to keep you from volunteering at the school."

"You mean infiltrating the ranks?" I have her interest.

"Exactly, Sherlock."

"What's the objective, Ranger?"

"To flesh out the 'alcohol' problem at the school, and to find out who targeted Sarah, and why."

"I'll be in the principal's office tomorrow, Mark, and thanks."

"Come in, please, Mrs. Garrison."

"I'm still not used to being in the principal's office."

"Did you spend a lot of time there?"

"More than I wanted, but this is different, I guess."

"How so? Please have a seat."

"I've got spare time when Sarah's in school. Do you need volunteers?"

"Does the sun rise in the East? When can you start?"

"What would I be doing?"

"Right now we have vacancies for aides in the special needs classes. Do you think you could do that?"

"I'm willing to try."

"There are some forms for you to complete and I'll need to speak with the teachers. Why don't you work on the forms and we'll get you started when you're ready, perhaps this week."

Lauren waits until we're all at the dinner table before springing her good news, or what seems to me like good news. "I'm going to volunteer some time at Sarah's school, possibly starting this week."

"I think that's great, honey," I say.

Sarah lets the news sink in before speaking. "Can I be excused?"

"Is something wrong?" I ask, and get THE glance. Sarah gets excused. Lauren follows Sarah. I stare at the pork chops.

Sarah is stretched out across her bed face down when Lauren comes into her room. "I thought you guys trusted me," Sarah says, rolling onto her back.

"Of course, we trust you. Is that what you think this is all about?"

"Why else would you volunteer at my school? Are you afraid I'll drink another mug of booze?"

"Of course not, Sarah, the school is the logical place for me to do part-time volunteering. We'll be off on the same days, that's all." That isn't all, but Sarah doesn't need to know the rest.

"Are you sure?"

"I'm sure."

"Some of the kids'll be uncomfortable with the ranger's wife around. They might think you're checking up on them, or that you don't trust me."

"I'll be working with special needs kids. That way I won't be where you are. Besides, there are only six more weeks of school this year. If it doesn't work, I'll be a greeter at Wal-Mart instead."

They're laughing when they join me at the dinner table, but both Lauren and I know that this is going to be a delicate balancing act.

CHAPTER 7

▼

With Lauren on Sarah's case, at least unofficially, I focus more intently on the homicide. I have a gut feeling that somehow the cases are connected and that alcohol is the catalyst. Was the previous Kisatchie death also alcohol-related?

Pete has no answer. "It was ruled a probable homicide by the previous ME, but the investigation was full of holes. Before the ME could reach a conclusion, the girl's badly decomposed body was released for cremation. There was so little evidence at the scene and, like the case of Ms. Beckett, we had little past history on the victim. The case went cold." Pete lifts his hands in resignation.

"Who interfered with the ME's investigation?"

"I wouldn't say that anyone interfered. Like I said, the body had been submerged in Bayou Pierre for weeks before someone or something dragged it onto the shoulder of the road. The family insisted that it be cremated, and Emil convinced us all that it was the proper thing to do. The ME was only too happy to see the case go away."

"Was a tox screen done?"

"Want to see the file?"

"Thought you'd never ask." I take the file into the back room and spread it out on a table, pour a cup of coffee, and don't come up for air until Pete asks me to lock up when I leave. It's after nine. There's no mention of a tox screen or preserved tissue samples. I note the girl's name, Lovely Hampden, and her parent's phone number in Jackson, Mississippi.

Normally, this isn't the kind of conversation one should have over the phone and I don't usually call people after nine, but time is getting away from me. To make matters worse, I'm fishing in very shallow waters, but I have a burning suspicion that this girl's death is somehow connected with the death of Ms. Beckett, Sarah's episode, and possibly the other "alcohol incidents" at the school.

Her mother answers the phone. After identifying myself and carefully establishing my purpose, I ask, "Can you think of any way that I could get a tissue sample of your daughter—possibly from her hair comb or brush, or her toothbrush or some clothing?" I hold my breath.

"In fact, there is," she says, "but why would you want it?" I'm sure she can hear me exhaling.

"It might help in an investigation of another death in the same place where your daughter died, and it might help in solving your daughter's case."

"She had the most beautiful hair, and hair, you know, takes a long time to die. They couldn't do much to prepare her for a funeral, you know. She was in pretty bad shape, but they washed and combed her hair, bless their hearts. I asked them to just snip a bit of it for me to keep. They were very kind. My husband kept telling me to hush, but they cut off a few inches, and placed it into a nice red envelope. It sits on her dresser in front of her high school picture. It's all that's left, you know. She really is, was a beautiful girl before … well, before she took to alcohol."

"I have a very difficult question to ask, Ma'am. Could you possibly spare a few strands of her hair for testing purposes?" Before I can continue, she interrupts.

"Oh, of course, they cut off more than I really need. Just tell me where to send it. I hope it helps. You sound like such a nice young man." I want to hug her. She promises to send the hair the next day.

"I'm going to call my father," Lauren says, after Sarah goes to bed.

"Hi Dad." He's at Millie's. I motion for her to put the phone on speaker.

"Hi, honey," Ace replies. "In case you haven't figured it out, I've moved into Millie's place, or should I say Mark's place?"

"It's both, Ace," I say, "but I thought you and Millie were going to wait until you got married?"

"We are, Ranger. I'm upstairs, she's down, and, by the way, it's not illegal."

"We're very happy for you, Dad."

"Sarah, too?" he asks. Dads know everything.

"Sarah, too."

"You got my letter, I take it. What do you think about our plans?"

"Actually, Dad, I like your plans, but I'd rather you come down here for the wedding. We all miss you."

"You sound anxious. Is everything okay?" The pause lasts too long. "What's going on? Give it to me straight."

"Nothing we can't handle, Dad."

"There's not much you can't handle, baby girl. Now, stop snowing your old man."

"Sarah's had a few bumps on the road to getting settled, and Mark isn't getting all the help he needs."

"He needs me and my Annie Oakley," Millie says. "Hope you don't mind that we went on speaker, too."

"Not now that you're family, Millie."

"Thanks, Lauren. Are you okay with that?"

"We want what's best for you both, Millie."

Ace jumps in. "You know we're both retired. Nothing to do but tend the garden, as they say. Our plans are written in sand. What would you have us do?"

"Well, I've been thinking how nice it would be if you could come down here for the wedding. I know your friends are there and you want Donna to do the service, but we have connections with a Lutheran minister here and I'm sure he'd be happy to help."

"We're Methodists, Lauren. Can Lutherans get along with Methodists?"

"You'd be surprised, Dad. They're not as standoffish as they seem. We'd love for you to come soon and get married here. Mark can't really get away until his business is finished."

"It's a done deal, right, Millie?" They cover the phone and discuss the decision—a good sign.

"Millie and I agree. Do you have room for us at your place?"

"Millie can use our third bedroom. You can sleep on the couch until the wedding."

"Now who's the parent?"

"I'm Sarah's parent. And you're her grandfather. Let's keep it proper for her sake."

"It's proper now. Millie wouldn't have it any other way."

"I'm proud of both of you. Let us know your travel plans. Try to come by way of the Natchez Trace Parkway. You'll love it."

I take the envelope containing several strands of Lovely Hampden's hair to Pete's office. "I need to have these tested to see if the victim was intoxicated when she died. Her mother said that she had 'taken to alcohol.' If she was drunk when she died there may be a connection to Ms. Beckett's death. We may be looking for a serial killer."

Pete interrupts. "You're taking quite a leap, Mark. First, I don't know for sure that they can tell what was in the girl's system at the time of her death by examining her hair, but I'm willing to ask. I'll send the hair to the lab in Shreveport. Second, we haven't established that the first victim died as a result of a homicide. You'll have a deuce of a time making the connection."

"Humor me, Pete. I have a gut feeling that alcohol plays into the deaths and the incidents at Sarah's school."

"Incidents? What incidents?"

"Hasn't Emil or the sheriff told you what's going on there?"

"You mean about Sarah?"

"Not just Sarah."

"Apparently not. Remember, it's not our jurisdiction." I repeat what I heard from the principal and the policeman at the hospital, but I don't mention that Lauren has volunteered to work at the school. Don't want to wake a snake to kill it.

"I'll let you know what I learn about the hair," Pete says. He doesn't sound enthusiastic. I leave the office and head for Roberval. It's time to get some answers from Constable Lachine.

I'm driving just under forty-five when I pass the money bush. Lachine's shiny Roberval vehicle is just beyond the s-curve in the center of town. I pull into a gas station parking lot and cross the street. Emil nods in my direction. "Hello, Ranger. Clocked you at forty-six, but I'll give you a pass."

"It's true then what they say about cops looking out for each other." He smiles.

"What brings you to my honey hole?"

"I come as a father, not a ranger, Emil. What is the disposition of the boys who urged alcohol on my daughter?"

"Disposition? Are you assuming something? The boys say they didn't force your daughter to drink anything, that she drank it on her own."

"These kids are in middle school, Emil. Have they been charged with possession by minors?"

"It's a little awkward here, Ranger. You see, they say your daughter brought the alcohol to school. Is there anyone who can say otherwise?"

"There was a witness."

"Yeah, I know, but she can't remember much one way or the other. Seems like a dead end to me. I warned those boys to watch their step, but there's not much else I can do. All three of the boys were suspended for three days from school, but I understand your daughter didn't get a suspension. Does that seem right to you? I mean, she was the one who was drinking." If his soft tone of voice wasn't so damned accusatory, I'd accept his logic, but he was shifting all the blame to Sarah.

"I'm going to tell you something, Emil. Sarah hasn't had a drink of alcohol in her entire life until the day she nearly died. Those boys played on her loneliness to get her to drink their liquor. What they did was not only illegal, but dangerous."

"Ranger, it's not always possible to tell when kids drink these days. They're pretty good at hiding it. You may be wrong about Sarah. I hope not, but one thing is sure. I can't make charges without evidence. I'm sorry about what happened to your daughter, but there's nothing more that I can do." Or that he's willing to do. I return to my SUV and go home.

"Put me on speaker," the caller said. The boys complied, as they were accustomed to doing. "If you two open your mouths to the ranger, you'll be choking on swamp water, understand?" They nodded to the telephone. "You stick with the story that the girl brought the booze and everything'll be just fine. Now, keep doing your work and I'll see that you're taken care of." The line went dead. Both boys stood watching the phone as if it had eyes, then the older boy hung it up.

"Guess what," Lauren says as I walk into the kitchen.

"Sarah's got plans for the evening. We'll be alone in the house. I'll pour the wine," I reply.

"Listen to me, you sex maniac. I got an e-mail from Dad today. They're coming here and plan to be married in Natchitoches."

"Better get the Lutheran pastor on board."

"No need. Guess who's going to meet them here?"

"I'm not in the mood for guessing games."

"Dave and Donna! And she's going to do the wedding here—in Natchitoches!"

"Dave and Donna?"

"They're dropping their kids off at Donna's parents and coming to Louisiana for a vacation! Can you believe it?"

My mind goes into a spin. It's been almost a month since we left New Hampshire. I miss Dave and the fellowship we had working together on the Appalachian Trail. And if Sarah sees Ace and Millie together perhaps she'll accept Millie as a grandmother-figure. "This is great news. We'll have to focus our energies on preparing for the wedding."

"No way, Ranger. You have crimes to solve. Stay out of my way. Finally, I have something exciting to keep me busy. Sarah will be pleased—I'll have to defer volunteering at the school."

"AUTO ACCIDENT KILLS TWO" read the headlines. "Two middle school students were killed when their car careened off of Texas 21 and wrapped around a tree. Neither youngster was wearing a safety belt. Both were underage, unlicensed, and had a blood alcohol level more than double the legal limit. The car belonged to the father of one of the boys." Neither boy is named in the article.

"What kind of father would permit middle school students to drive?" I ask no one in particular at the breakfast table. Lauren shakes her head as she reads the article over my shoulder.

"Not all parents are cops," Sarah says with a smile. She probably doesn't realize that this is the first direct reference she has made to me as her parent. I accept the connection, inadvertent or not. "I wonder who they are. No one has called."

Sarah's involvement in the Lutheran youth group and her ballet class has expanded her social network. The phone is becoming a little more active in our apartment. The fact that she doesn't know who the boys are probably means that they aren't among her new friends.

"Let's turn on the radio," I suggest. Local news is mute on naming the boys, but reports that classes at the middle school for periods one and two have been cancelled and that there will be counselors available for any students or parents who wish to see them. I don't fully understand this new procedure, although as a law enforcement officer, having participated in some first responder training, I know it's important for people impacted by a traumatic event to talk about it afterward. Supposedly, it reduces the possibility of post traumatic stress syndrome. "Do you want to meet with a counselor, Sarah?" She shakes her head.

"I'd like to get to school on time, though, so I can talk to Lonnie. His Dad'll know what's going on." She's probably right. Emil will have listened to his scanner and will be at the school, especially since there was alcohol involved.

"I'll take you to school this morning. Anyway, your mother has a lot of organizing to do for the wedding." Not surprisingly, there are policemen and reporters lingering around the school entrance. No one is being admitted into the school building except those seeing counselors. Sarah disappears with her friends in search of Lonnie while I park the Excursion and walk to the entrance, hoping to find Emil.

The principal greets me coolly. I'm not surprised after Sarah's experience and my follow-up inquiries; nevertheless, I smile and extend my hand. "Have you seen Constable Lachine?" He points to the parking lot, and then directs a father and son into the building. "Thanks," I say to his back. I head for Emil who's engaged in a lively and animated conversation with three young men in the parking lot. When he sees me coming, the group disperses. I expect the boys to turn toward the school, but instead they squeeze into a pickup truck and drive out of the parking lot.

"Out of your territory, aren't you, Ranger?"

"I have a daughter that attends school here, Emil. I drove her this morning. Do you have a problem with that?"

"No problem. Just a little on edge, I guess. The accident last night is going to put the heat on our alcohol issue."

"Just what is our alcohol problem, Emil?"

"Too many kids doing too much drinking, that's all."

"It seems like an access problem to me. Where are they getting it?"

"Probably at home."

"Have we asked the parents? Isn't this primarily a Baptist community? They aren't drinkers, are they?"

"You still crossing boundaries, Ranger? Isn't this a civilian matter?"

"Two teens have died in the national forest, at least one of whom was intoxicated. That makes my interest professional, not to mention the assault on my daughter here at school."

"Assault? What assault?"

"Have you forgotten that she almost died as a result of alcohol poisoning?"

"You said that two teens died in the forest. I know about the Beckett girl. Who was the other?"

"Her name was Lovely Hampden." Lachine's face pales. His usually agile mind goes into lockdown. It takes a full thirty seconds for him to respond. Fortunately for him, my mobile phone rings at the end of his brain pause. "You'll have to excuse me," I say. He's pleased to oblige. We go our separate ways.

The caller is the sheriff of Caddo Parish, but he has hung up. His message on my voice mail informs me that the finger print tests on the gas can have been processed and the report can be faxed to my office or picked up in Shreveport. I reply, opting for the latter.

CHAPTER 8

▼

"Guess what?" Sarah asks, bursting through the side door into the kitchen.

"What?" says Lauren.

"The boys who died in the so-called accident last week may have been murdered."

"I know. I heard it on the radio this afternoon. Who told you?"

"Lonnie. His dad said they were probably too drunk to drive."

"The Natchitoches Parish sheriff's office made the same statement to the press. Texas authorities have started an investigation."

That makes four and almost five, I think. Beckett, Hampden, these two boys, and Sarah—all victims of alcohol overdose. Someone is pouring booze into these kids.

"I've got news in a lighter vein," Lauren says. "Dad and Millie left today for their trip to Louisiana. Dad also emailed the flight information for Dave and Donna. They're flying to Shreveport. I told them you'd pick them up."

"Not a problem. In fact, I've got to see Sheriff Hardman in Shreveport."

"Who's Sheriff Hardman?" Sarah asks.

"He's the sheriff of Caddo Parish. He has some information for me. When are the Kraft's arriving?"

"On Monday. They'll be here for a week, and there's more. The wedding will be at the Lutheran Church. I called the pastor and he said the church is available on Saturday. He'll be away, but the property man will open and close the building. He has no problem with Donna conducting the wedding. See, Lutherans and Methodists can get along."

"I might be able to get some friends from the youth group to help, Mom. We could make coffee for afterwards."

"That's great, Sarah." It's her first show of enthusiasm for her grandfather's wedding. Sarah's coming along.

"Ever try to get prints off an old gas can?" Sheriff Hardman asks as he escorts me into his office. Military and government offices are functional, to put it politely, but Hardman's is more like a suite. No counters with desk sergeants holding court. Visitors are greeted by a well-groomed and well-spoken middle-aged lady who records your name and time of arrival, then directs you to living room furniture arranged around a coffee table. No clipboards shoved across the desk or stained mugs half full of cold coffee. This table includes French vanilla creamers, stirrers, and napkins. To complete the surprise, I'm not kept waiting. No sooner than I'm handed fresh coffee with French vanilla creamer stirred to the right consistency am I escorted into the sheriff's suite.

Hardman takes his position behind a polished cherry desk large enough for a Thanksgiving dinner. He extends his hand and we greet one another. The sheriff is affable, a necessary trait for a lawman whose job is more political than functional. He takes a paper from his drawer and directs me toward a setting of leather furniture to the right of his desk. I feel like I'm in a gentlemen's club. I wait for his secretary to bring cigars. "There are more prints on that old can than you want to hear about, but very few are readable."

"Any matches on the good prints?"

"Yep, several—yours, of course, then a couple more government folks—your supervisor Toussant, a man named Lachine, and Lauren Adams. You know these people?"

"Lachine is the constable in Roberval. Lauren Adams, a former deputy sheriff in New Hampshire, is now Lauren Adams Garrison, my wife. None of these names surprise me. They all had access to the gas can."

"The request form said that this can is part of an investigation of an attempt on your life, Ranger Garrison. Want to elaborate?"

"Someone tried to dump Lauren and me into Toledo Bend Reservoir—without a paddle, so to speak."

"Great bass fishing, but a lousy place for a swim."

"Holes were drilled through the bottom of the boat, and the gas can was emptied and placed over the holes. Someone wanted us swamped, stalled, and probably silenced."

"Heavy charges, Ranger."

"Give me another theory."

"Got your point. What else can I do to help?" He sounds genuinely concerned.

"I'm not sure, but I'd like to keep in touch. Thanks for your help on the gas can." I stand, expecting to leave. He remains seated.

"You folks have a problem down there, don't you?"

"Exactly which problem are you referring to?"

"Your local sheriff has some rum-running going on, I hear."

"Rum-running?"

"Unlicensed liquor sales. Avoids taxes. Probably sold to underage drinkers."

Unwittingly, Sheriff Hardman gives me what I'm looking for. My suspicions about alcohol being at the center of the problems in the Kisatchie investigations are confirmed, but I don't have enough pieces to begin putting the puzzle together.

It's way too early to meet Dave and Donna at the airport, so I drive to the Bass Pro Shop in Bossier City to wander through the aisles and daydream. In the main entrance, high on a shelf above the customer service desk, a stuffed puma catches my eye. I've heard that the puma population is increasing rapidly in Louisiana, especially in the forests. They're coming in from the eastern part of Texas and from as far away as Florida. As their natural habitat diminishes in those areas, they turn to heavily-forested Louisiana. These big cats are causing problems for cattle and sheep farmers. Dog owners are also on the alert. "Big rascals aren't they?" a sales clerk says from behind me.

"Yes they are. We didn't run into these on the Appalachian Trail."

"From the East, I take it."

"Yep. Tell me about these cats."

"I can't tell you much, but that lady over there is an expert. She records reliable sightings for the parish animal control office." He points to a woman standing near the door to the gun department. A forest ranger should know about the critters in the forest, so I approach the lady with the same question.

"These cats aren't new to Louisiana. They've been here for a long time, but the population is increasing rapidly, and they're getting braver—coming closer to residential areas, especially where hounds are kept. Hunters and farmers are watching for them. Bobcats and coyotes are also on the increase. They like Louisiana because our main crop is pine lumber, so there is plenty of forest habitat."

"Is the stuffed cat at the entrance typical?"

"Not at all. That one is a female. They're considerably smaller than males which run up to eight feet in length and weigh as much as 250 pounds. The one at the entrance is about six feet and less than 150 pounds. We call them pumas around here, but they're also called mountain lions, cougars, panthers, and other local names. Although the color of the cats differs according to region, they all have some common markings—black on the sides of their muzzle and on the backs of their ears. The throat and neck are almost always whitish. Young ones are spotted, but lose their spots in adulthood.

"What is their prey?"

"Amazingly, everything from ground mammals to full grown cattle, even horses and burros. This is why livestock farmers are on the lookout for them."

"What about people?"

"They deserve our respect. They are amazing jumpers. They can make a running long jump greater than 45 feet, and can leap vertically up to 15 feet. They're great stalkers and usually claim their prey in two or three leaps."

"Are they found in groups?"

"They're loners and they don't dispute over territory or females. They get along and respect each other's territory."

We talk a bit longer about ways to recognize their dens, and, after thanking the lady, I make my way through the aisles of fishing and hunting gear, and guns that I'll never be able to afford. The cell phone interrupts my day dreaming. It's Dave Kraft.

"Where are you, Ranger Garrison? Weren't you going to pick us up?"

"For crying out loud, Dave! What's going on? You weren't supposed to be here for another hour."

"Our plane arrived early. That's what phones are for. Didn't you check the arrival schedule?"

"Tell me where to pick you up. I'm only twenty minutes from the airport." I have totally goofed and will not hear the end of it from Lauren or Donna.

Dave and Donna are at the arrival curb. We share hugs, load their bags into the Excursion, and head south on I-49. Dave looks good—tanned, trim, and not a day older than when we left New England five weeks earlier. Donna looks like she's ready for a vacation. Serving a small Methodist church as sole pastor, and raising a young family is difficult work, especially for a type-a personality who also has an artificial leg. Dave climbs into the front passenger seat, and Donna stretches out behind us. "Tired?" I ask over my shoulder.

"Exhausted," she says. "We've been in every airport between New England and the Gulf Coast."

"It wasn't that bad," Dave counters. "We flew out of Manchester to avoid the Logan mess. There are no direct flights from Manchester to Shreveport, as one might guess. Three takeoffs and landings up the odds for a calamity, but here we are, safe and sound."

"The itinerary that Ace emailed shows stops in Oklahoma City and Dallas, right?"

"Right," says Donna. "But there weren't long enough stopovers to see any of the sights, so we just went from plane to plane. It's been a long day."

"How far is Natchitoches from Shreveport?" Dave asks.

"About sixty-five miles, and you need to know how to pronounce the name of the city. It's pronounced na'-ku-dish. It's got an interesting history, which you'll learn when we see the sights. For starters, it's the oldest town in the Louisiana Purchase."

"Great. What I really want to hear about is you and how you're doing on your case."

"Are you sure, Dave? You're on vacation."

"I'm sure." I look in the mirror to see whether we'll be boring Donna, but she's already asleep.

It takes most of the trip to fill Dave in on the Kisatchie deaths, Sarah's episode, and the auto deaths of the boys. He's more interested in the attempt on Lauren's and my life at Toledo Bend Reservoir. I have no answers or suspicions. "Somehow I've touched a nerve. I know I've made the local constable nervous by poking around after Sarah's event, but I think we've worked that out."

"Is there any common ground here, Mark?"

"I think so. In some way, alcohol is playing a role in all of these events. I visited the sheriff of Caddo Parish before I picked you up at the airport. He casually mentioned that there's a problem in our area with what he referred to as 'rum-running.'"

"Rum-running? Is liquor illegal in Louisiana?"

"Liquor laws vary from parish to parish which makes rum-running an opportunity for those wishing to transport and sell untaxed liquor."

"Do people still do that?"

"I'm going to find out. That may be one of the missing pieces in my puzzle."

"What's that?" Donna asks from the backseat.

"Welcome back to the world," Dave says. "What's what?"

"I just saw the weirdest thing on the side of the road. It looked like a wrinkled football."

"It was probably an armadillo," I say. "They're not too swift, they get run over. You'll see more of them in Texas. Welcome to the South."

"Do you like it down here, Mark?" Donna asks. I couldn't tell by the tone of her voice which answer she was expecting, but I suspect that she wasn't planning to move south yet.

"It's different, takes some getting used to. It grows on you. Sarah and Lauren are ready to return to New England, but that's their base. They're homesick. We're not acclimated yet, I guess. Anyway, our likes and dislikes are irrelevant just now. We have a job to do."

"Maybe I can help you do it, Mark," says Dave.

"How's the leg, Donna?"

"Hardly know it isn't mine."

"You should see her; she doesn't miss a beat—does everything she used to do. These new prosthetics are amazing."

"Well, not everything, Dave. You exaggerate. Bikinis are out."

"I'm proud of you, Donna," I say. Judy would have been proud, too, I think. Donna's survival and recovery from the explosion that killed Judy has been a real miracle.

"Are we going to go by the Kisatchie?" Dave asks.

"It's beyond Natchitoches, Dave. I know Lauren and Sarah are anxious to see you guys, but, if you'd like, we can take an extra half hour and drive through the forest."

"I'd like."

I pass the Natchitoches turnoff at the San Antonio Trace and continue southeast to Route 119, the road that takes us past Bayou Pierre. As I pull to the side of the road to point out the exact location where the girls' bodies were found, Dave and Donna are glued to their windows. Although Dave has been a ranger longer than I have, he has little experience with violent crime, but shows both interest and aptitude for this kind of work. I avoid sharing graphic details about the homicides for Donna's sake, waiting for a time when Dave and I will be alone. We then drive leisurely along the Longleaf Trail Scenic Byway admiring the spring flowers.

"Look," she says as we pass the entrance to the Caroline Dormon Trail, popular with horse owners. "Can we do some riding while we're here?"

"Is that possible with …"

"Karen?" Donna interrupts. "That's the name I've given my leg, Mark."

"Why Karen?"

"Because a girl we both know named Karen overcame many hardships to make a good life. It's named after her."

"Okay. Can you and Karen ride a horse?"

"Just wait and see."

CHAPTER 9

▼

Sarah and Lauren get a kick out of painting a "welcome" banner for Dave and Donna which they hang on the side of the apartment building. After a round of hugs, Dave and I unload luggage while the girls make kitchen talk.

"Is this our Sarah?" Donna asks as Sarah comes out of her bedroom. More hugs. Dave and Sarah exchange nods. Formalities over, Sarah turns to me.

"Dad," she says, which immediately warms my heart. I glance quickly at Lauren and catch her smile. "You need to hear this."

"Okay, I'm all ears."

"You know the boys that died in the car in Texas?"

"Yes."

"It's all over school."

"What's all over school?" She's nearly panting to tell the whole story.

"It's definite now. They were murdered."

"How do you know this?"

"Lonnie told me, but he asked me to keep it to myself. They were dead before the so-called accident. Someone else crashed the car to make it look like an accident—and, guess what?"

"Go on." She has my wheels turning.

"They went to my school. One of them was part of the group that, well ..."

"Made you sick?"

"Uh-huh."

The Forest Service owns four horses that are kept stabled at the Fort Polk Wildlife Management Area. The stable manager is delighted when I arrange for

Donna and Lauren to take two horses to the Kisatchie for a trail ride. He will arrange to have the trailer and gear ready when the women arrive. "They just don't get enough exercise," he says. He agrees to lend me a hitch for my receptacle so that Lauren can tow the trailer with my Excursion. Everything is in order on Tuesday morning for their ride on the Caroline Dormon Trail.

Dave and I sip coffee as they leave to get their horses. "Why Fort Polk?" Dave asks.

"The WMA is a great outdoor sports area—hunting and fishing, and not only for the folks stationed at Ft. Polk. It's open in season for the general public. Rules are fairly strict, I'm told, but the wildlife population is abundant. They also cooperate with the Forest Service in several ways, like stabling our horses."

"What would you like to do while you're here, Dave?"

"The word is out about Toledo Bend Reservoir. I'm told it's a great bass lake, yes?"

"Yes, fishermen from everywhere come down here. It's a bit treacherous because of the stickups, but the fish are in there. Do you want to give it a try?"

"Must you ask?"

"What would you say if we wait for Ace? He's a fisherman."

"Sounds like a winner. You skirted the details about your investigation yesterday, Mark, for Donna's sake, I assume. How about filling me in?"

"I haven't made much progress on the homicides, Dave, but here's what I know. Two girls' bodies were found in Bayou Pierre. The first was found over a year ago and the case went cold. The second was found several months ago. Alcohol seems to have played a role in their deaths. We know that the Beckett girl, the second victim, had an extremely high level of alcohol in her blood. I'm waiting for the result of tests on the hair of the first victim. Why they wound up in Bayou Pierre is a mystery."

"Why did the first case go cold?"

"The ME was encouraged to release the decomposed body early for cremation—before any tests were done. Just bad police work, I'd say. There is a rather laid back attitude down here, Dave. I'm not in tune with it."

"How'd you get hair to test?" I told him about my conversation with Lovely Hampden's mother.

"Dave, I don't want to see you get involved in all of this on your vacation. Why don't I get you over to the marina by the bridge where you can rent a boat and do some fishing? I'd arrange for the Forest Service boat, but it's evidence in my investigation, as you know, and has a few unfriendly holes in the hull."

"There's time for fishing, Mark. What's the possibility of meeting your supervisor—Toussant?"

"He goes by Pete. Are you sure it's what you want to do?" Dave nods.

We pedal Lauren and Sarah's bikes to the Forest Service office. Pete's vehicle is in front of the building. He's on the phone, but sees us enter the building and motions for us to wait outside his office, closing the door. After a few minutes, he invites us in. As usual, his desk is cleared and he's neatly uniformed. "Pete, this is my former partner on the Appalachian Trail, Dave Kraft."

"Dave, welcome to Louisiana. I'm Pete Toussant. I understand you're here for the wedding."

"And an overdue vacation—hopefully to include some fishing."

"I hope you enjoy both. I'm not a fisherman, but I hear good things about Toledo Bend." Turning to me, he says, "Tell Lauren that I'll be at the wedding, Mark. Thanks for including me. I hate to mix business with pleasure, but I'd like a brief update on your investigation."

Somehow I thought it was *our* investigation, but I let his choice of words slide. "Deliberate is the only word that fits, Pete. I can't get past the idea that we're dealing with an alcohol issue. Just how it fits together with the deaths in the Kisatchie I don't yet know, but I'll keep you informed. Incidentally, have you received any word on Lovely Hampden's hair?"

"Oh, didn't you get the message I left on your answering machine? The results came a few days ago." He removes an envelope from the center drawer of his desk and hands it to me.

"I'll go over this later, Pete." I begin to put the envelope in my pocket, but Pete reaches for it.

"I'd like to keep the records together, Mark, if you don't mind."

"I'll just make a copy then, Pete."

"The machine's not working right now, Mark. I'll see that you get one."

"Then I'll take a minute to read it." Before handing the envelope back to Pete I open the report. The hair study reveals the presence of alcohol in Lovely's body along with several compounds that I don't recognize. I return the report to Pete and we leave his office. Passing through the clerk's area I notice that the copy machine is turned on.

Dave has a puzzled look on his face as we get on our bikes. "What's up, Dave?"

"Before I called your cell phone from the airport, I tried reaching you at your apartment. No one answered and I didn't get a message from your answering machine."

"I don't have one."

The Caroline Dormon Trail is ten and a half miles long and is used by hikers, bikers, and horseback riders. I passed the trailhead several times on my rides along the Longleaf Scenic Byway, but never hiked the trail. I'm anxious to hear about Lauren and Donna's experience. Be careful what you're anxious for. The phone is ringing in the kitchen as Dave and I return from Pete's office.

"Ranger Garrison."

"Oh, good, I've been trying to get you for the past hour. I'm a volunteer at Kisatchie. There's been an accident." My heart stops beating.

"Go on, please. What's happened?" Dave is now paying attention.

"Is Lauren your wife?"

"Yes, go on, please."

"She and Donna Kraft were riding horses on the Dormon Trail …" I thought, Oh, God, no, not again. "Ms. Kraft's horse was spooked by something and threw her. She's been taken by ambulance to the hospital."

"How badly is she hurt?"

"Not badly. Please don't panic. The rescue folks thought she needed to be checked out, that's all."

"Where's my wife right now?"

"As far as I know, Mrs. Garrison is taking the horses back to Polk and is going to go to the hospital. We don't get cell phone service out here, so I'm sure she'll call you when she's in range. You might want to go to the hospital."

"Okay. Thanks." I hang up and repeat the conversation for Dave. "We'd better get going."

"Going where? To which hospital?"

"To the hospital in Natchitoches. I'll call there."

"Rev. Kraft is waiting for transfer to a room," I'm told.

"Where is the hospital?"

"Cross the river on Pine St., go east and follow the hospital signs. Park in the visitor's lot, not the emergency lot." I thank her, and then remember that I don't have a car.

"Should I call a cab?" Dave asks.

"We'll be there before the taxi."

"Let's go." It takes twenty minutes.

Donna is on a gurney in the hallway of the general medical floor waiting for a room to be assigned. I can see a void where Karen should have been. This isn't good. The only visible wounds are some scratches on the arm that's not covered.

"Honey, what happened?" Dave asks as he takes her visible hand in his.

"Don't worry, Dave. It's nothing, really. We had a wonderful ride—almost to the end of the trail. I don't know what it was that spooked Caramel, but he kicked out and I went down. I think Karen is damaged. I know my leg is injured, but superficially. I got a little scratched up when I fell, but nothing serious, really."

"Then, why are you here?"

"Because the orthopedist on duty wants to make sure that Karen and I get back together again."

"Will you be admitted?"

"I've already been admitted. It may take awhile before Karen and I get the treatment we need. They have to send her to Jackson. In the meantime, I'll be back on crutches." She turns to me. "Lauren is a saint, Mark. She led Caramel back to the trailer after they took me on an ATV stretcher kind of deal. When I was able to reach her by cell phone, she was on her way to the stable. That was about eleven o'clock. She should be here any minute. You can probably call her on your cell phone now that she's out of the woods." I do just that, but get a no signal reply. I try again in the parking lot. While I'm dialing, the Excursion comes into sight.

"I was just trying to call you, Lauren."

"Mark, I'm a mess. I need to find a place to get myself together. Is Donna okay?"

"I think so. I just left her and Dave. She seems to be in good spirits, but with minor injuries. It sounds as though Karen suffered the most."

"Karen was bent where legs shouldn't be bent."

"When you have yourself together, we'll talk. Why don't you go home and come back when you're ready. I'll stay here." She agrees. I load the bikes in the Excursion and she promises to return as soon as she can.

Dave is sitting in the visitor's section just outside the elevator doors on the general med floor. Donna's not in sight. "Is she in a room?" I ask.

"Yep. The orthopedist is with her. He said he'd give me an update after his exam. I just got off the phone with my supervisor. I'm now officially off of vacation and on family leave—for as long as it takes. She's a great supervisor."

"She?"

"Yep, it's a new world, Mark, but I love it. She's been in the Forest Service longer then I have, and has a great gift for managing people. Anyway, I'm not to return until Donna's ready."

"Welcome to Louisiana, Dave."

Dave and I are in the hospital cafeteria when Lauren finds us. "How's Donna?"

"Basically okay," Dave answers. "She has a hairline fracture of a wrist bone, and a severe bruise on her leg, which she refuses to call a stump. They've put her wrist in a restraint and iced her leg; otherwise, she's just scratched up in a few places. She's in great spirits, but misses Karen."

"How badly was Karen hurt?"

"Not beyond repair, but the nearest prosthetic supplier is in Jackson, Mississippi, so they'll be sending Karen out of state. We'll just have to wait for her to be repaired."

"Dave's on family leave now, Lauren, so they'll be staying for awhile."

"Great. That means I'll have a real adult to talk to during the day."

"Thanks," I say. "Let's go see the patient."

Donna is in a hospital gown sitting on the edge of her bed. She's the only patient in the semi-private room. Dave sits next to her. Lauren plops down on a chair and I stand a few steps back. Donna spreads her arms, turns her palms upward and motions for us to come closer. She guides us into a circle and bows her head. We take the cue and follow her lead. Her prayer is straight from the heart, thanking God that everyone is well and asking for quick and complete recovery. Lauren gives my hand a quick squeeze and we resume our former places.

"The ride was a bust, wasn't it, Lauren?"

"In more ways than one."

"Did you enjoy it as much as I did?"

"Under the circumstances, yes."

"Tell me what happened after they hauled me off."

"I led Caramel to the trailer. He acted like a real gentlemen. Both horses went into the trailer without complaint. The ride to Polk was a little anxious, not knowing your situation. What about you?"

"Once they got Karen off, I was okay—really. They put an ice pack on my leg, cleaned up the scratches, and put me on an ATV with a hammock-like stretcher—the kind they use in the military. They didn't return the way we had come, but used a service road to the Scenic Byway. It was a fairly smooth ride and the rescuers were really great. The only thing we saw along the way was an old barn. They put me in an ambulance when we got to the byway, and you know the rest. All this notwithstanding, Lauren, I had a great time riding and I'd love to do it again."

"How long do you expect to be here, Donna?" Dave asks.

"At least for the night. They'll probably release me in the morning if the x-rays of my leg are okay. You could do me a huge favor, Dave. They brought me a menu for dinner and nothing looked good. Could you get me some real food?"

"Dave," I say, "there's a place near here called The Crawfish Hole. You can walk there. You have to have crawfish while you're here, so why not take out a few dozen and have a real Louisiana feast right here in Donna's room? In fact, I'll drive you down there and bring you back, and then Lauren and I have to pick Sarah up at the ballet studio." Donna waves us off.

When I tell the girl at the pickup counter that we're taking the crawfish to the hospital, she makes a real production of the order, placing extra sauce, napkins, and French fries in the bag with the crustaceans. Dave's amazed at what he sees. Customers have piles of squeezed shells and beer pitchers on their picnic tables and are having a great time. "Think I can bring a pitcher of beer?" he asks with a smile.

"Not likely. I'd suggest something lighter." He orders a liter bottle of soda. I drop him off at the hospital entrance, not knowing whether they'll let him bring his messy feast into the room. Lauren and I head for the ballet studio.

Sarah is always up after a lesson at the studio. Although we can't really afford the lessons, the payoff is evident in the way Sarah carries herself, the friends she's made, and the attitude she brings home afterwards. She jumps up to the backseat and we head home after a very interesting day. I pull the Excursion into the drive-way and Lauren's the first one out. She goes to the kitchen door and backs away quickly. "What's wrong, Mom?" Sarah asks.

Lauren stops Sarah and me from moving toward the house. "Someone's inside," she says.

"How do you know?" I ask.

"I didn't leave the kitchen lights on."

"Did you lock the door when you came to the hospital?"

"I can't remember. I was in a hurry."

"Lauren, you and Sarah get into the Excursion, and back it out of the driveway. Stay there until I come for you." I walk back to the car, get my service pistol from the glove compartment, and return to the side door. After chambering a round, I follow the pistol carefully and quietly into the kitchen, looking in all directions. Nothing. Entering the living room, I see a familiar person rising from a reclining position on the couch.

"Put that dang thing down, Ranger, before I bop you with this cane. You wouldn't shoot an old lady, would you? You're darn lucky I left Annie Oakley at home!"

"Millie Disch, one of these days you're going to sneak up on me and get what you deserve. How'd you get in here, and where's that indiscriminate man who wants to marry you?"

"You left your door open, and my discerning fiancé is out looking for a drugstore to get me some aspirin. New England to whatever you call this place is a long trip for old people."

"You'll never get old, Millie," I say as I sit next to her on the couch, each of us reaching for a hug. "I have a pain killer of some sort, Millie. I'll get some for you, but first let me get Lauren and Sarah. They're hiding in the Excursion for fear of their lives."

"Before we get all chummy and share our stories, this old lady needs a nap."

"Not before you say hello." I step into the driveway and wave the girls inside, wondering how Sarah will greet Millie. I don't have long to wonder. There are hugs all around, but Millie remains seated on the couch. I wonder whether her hip replacement has ever healed completely, or if she is simply as tired as she says. She looks rested and is her spicy self.

"He's here! He's here!" Sarah interrupts as Ace pulls into the driveway, but it's Lauren who goes running.

I've been blind and deaf to Lauren's need for her father. This is a learning moment for me that will shape our future as a family. "Dad," Lauren says as she runs to greet her father. Ace embraces his daughter in a hug that doesn't want to end. Why hadn't I picked up on the intensity of this relationship? With his arm around her waist, they walk toward Sarah and me. Lauren is somewhere between laughing and crying. I guess it doesn't matter which as much as it shows her deep emotional bond with her father. I expect this from Sarah, but instead Sarah holds back until Ace comes close, then she gives her grandfather a kiss on the cheek. Is she uncertain about their relationship because of Millie? I have to pay closer attention to my family.

"Mark, how are you doing?" Ace asks as we all move in the direction of the living room to join Millie.

"Getting along," I say. "How was the drive?"

"Just great, but I'll fill everyone in at dinner. Millie and I want to take everyone out to a nice restaurant."

"I know just the place."

"Did we get here before the Kraft's?" Millie asks.

Lauren, still clinging to her father, takes a drink order, while Sarah gathers card table chairs. "Kraft's are here, but Donna's in the hospital and Dave's with her," I say.

"Oh, dear," says Millie. "What's happened?"

"Lauren will fill you in when everyone gets settled, but don't worry. She's okay."

Dave joins us as the sun is setting. "Donna's sleeping," he says. "She's expecting to be released tomorrow morning after the orthopedist sees her." Ace and Millie get settled into the Holiday Inn Express. Separate rooms until Saturday night, Millie assures us. I wonder if they're adjoining rooms.

The Landing, a restaurant with a view of the Cane River, is noted for its good food. It will be our first real social outing since arriving in Louisiana. Lauren and Sarah are primping in Sarah's room while Dave and I make plans for our fishing trip with Ace. We agree that it'll be our bachelor party for Ace. "There's a marina on the Texas side of the bridge where we can rent a boat. I don't have enough gear for three, but Pete may have some that we can borrow."

"Didn't he say he doesn't fish?" Dave asks.

"Right." We decide to take a trip to Wal-Mart.

"We'd better get going," Lauren says as she and Sarah step into the hallway. Lauren and Sarah haven't dressed up since our last meal in Natchez. Lauren's wearing a blouse that I haven't seen before, much to my regret. She looks tremendous. Sarah looks more like a young woman than a middle school student. I'm proud of my girls.

I spot Ace's rented car, a new orange Mustang convertible, parked on the street in front of The Landing. Ace and Millie are sitting on a bench near the river. Ace has his arm around Millie who's leaning into him. They look like high school kids on a date. Sarah and Lauren look in silence. I descend the steps from the street to the river bank, give Millie my arm, and we join the others on the sidewalk.

Over dinner Ace and Millie tell the story of their drive from New Hampshire to Natchitoches. They stopped in Nashville to do the tourist scene, then drove the Natchez Trace as we had suggested. After several days in Natchez, they headed west. We have much to share.

"What ever possessed you to rent a convertible?" I ask.

"Ever driven one?" Ace replies.

"Never."

"Then you wouldn't understand if I told you."

"Once you get used to bad hair days, they're a lot of fun," says Millie. "We're thinking about buying one when we get back to New England. Lauren, it's your turn to talk. Whatever happened to you and Donna to land that sweet little minister in the hospital?" Lauren tells the Caroline Dormon story. "Is she going to be able to hook me up with this old man on Saturday?" Everyone looks at Dave.

"Sure thing. She's fine, really. The doctor's being a little cautious because the leg has to be completely healed before Karen can be back in action."

"Karen?" Ace asks.

"The name Donna gave her artificial leg," Dave answers. "Don't ask. I'll pick Donna up tomorrow. It's doubtful that Karen will be back before Saturday, so Donna may have to do the wedding on crutches. Is that a problem?"

"If I can be married on a cane, she can do the marrying on a crutch," said Millie. "It's a wonder that Ace and I aren't driving down the aisle in electric wheelchairs, or whatever they call those things. Imagine being married at our ages, and me for the fourth time!"

"The wonder is that I'd marry a woman who's outlived three husbands already. It's a downright omen."

"They died happy," Millie says. "Anyway, I'd have no trouble finding a fifth with that new convertible."

"Okay, you guys," Lauren says. "Donna told me the rehearsal will be at the church on Friday evening, and then Mark and I are taking you out for a rehearsal dinner. The wedding is scheduled for 10:00 a.m. Saturday. What are your plans for leaving?"

"Don't they teach you manners in Louisiana?" Ace asks his daughter. "Already you're kicking us out?"

"You can stay as long as you like, Dad. I thought you'd be taking a honeymoon."

"We've discussed that. We can't think of a better honeymoon than being with you guys for awhile. We may slip down to New Orleans for a few days. Will we be getting in your way?"

"Never. The only thing is that we don't have room for everyone at the apartment."

"They can stay in my room," Sarah says. "I'll sleep on the couch, pleeeeese?"

"It's a done deal," I say. Sarah's face lights up and I think she's going to give me a hug. Maybe another time.

"Ace, Dave and I would like to talk about a fishing trip—maybe Thursday?"

CHAPTER 10

▼

After dinner, Ace and Millie go to their hotel, Dave goes to the hospital, and the Garrison family goes home—Sarah to bed, and Lauren to the living room couch while I pour two glasses of white Port. "When will Dave be back?" she asks.

"When I pick him up. He's on foot."

"Do you mean we have the house to ourselves?"

"What about Sarah?"

"She's sleeping."

"You really look great in that outfit. Should I put on some music?"

"Yes, something soft." I put on a Tony Bennett CD and we fold into one another, swaying to the slow beat. How long has it been? Between tracks we sip Port. After "I Left My Heart in San Francisco" we stop dancing altogether and stand, locked in an embrace. I pull her blouse over her head, unsnap her bra and let it fall to the floor. She drops her skirt, takes my hand and leads me to the bedroom. Everything is perfect. After making love, we lay in each others arms waiting for Dave's call. "I love you, Mark," she whispers.

"I love you, Lauren, more than I can say." The phone rings as expected.

Dave is waiting in front of the hospital when I arrive. "Everything on track for Donna's release tomorrow?"

"Yep. I'll need to borrow your car, Mark."

"I need to see Pete tomorrow. You should probably rent a car, Dave."

"No problem."

"I'll take you to the rental agency. Then, why don't you take Donna on a tour of Natchitoches? She'd probably like that. She's been cooped up for awhile."

"What's to see?"

"Actually, it's a very historical place. I'll give you a map of the Cane River area. Did you know that 'Sweet Magnolias' was filmed here? She might enjoy a horse-drawn tour of the town."

"What will you be doing tomorrow?"

"Work. I have an investigation going, you know."

"Will I miss out on anything?"

"A few front teeth if you spend the day with me and not your wife. You're on vacation, you know, and besides, doesn't she have some wedding planning to take care of?"

"She's been working on that in the hospital. The Lutheran pastor even came by to see how she was doing and discuss the wedding. She's ready to visit and relax."

Lauren is in bed when I bring Dave home. She's made his bed and left a snack for him in the kitchen. I say good night and get into bed with my naked wife. We fall asleep in each other's arms.

Two things that bother me require input from Pete. Sheriff Hardman reported clear prints on the gas can from Lauren, Emil, Pete, and me. Three of the prints are understandable. Emil, an excellent fisherman, has used the boat on a number of occasions. Lauren and I handled the gas can, but if Pete doesn't fish, why are his prints there? Second, why didn't I know about the barn in the Kisatchie? Pete should have answers.

"How's the party going?" Pete asks when I walk into the office. He's at the copier.

"Which party?" I ask.

"At your place." He doesn't ask about the investigation.

"Everyone arrived safely, and the wedding plans are on track."

"How's Dave's wife?" Had I mentioned Donna's accident?

"Dave's taking her home from the hospital as we speak."

"Happened on the Dormon, yes?"

"Right."

"Did they have a good ride?"

"Until she was thrown."

"What did they say about the ride?"

"Donna talked mostly about the rescue, but she did say that she saw a barn in the forest. I didn't know there was a barn. Were there occupants or workers there when Ms. Beckett's body was found? Were they questioned about it?"

"Whoa, slow down. There's nothing to get excited about." I wonder if there's anything that excites Pete. "It's an old barn, that's all."

Pete doesn't seem to know much about the barn, so I make a mental note to check it out for myself. "I'll stop by there when I can." Pete doesn't respond. "I'm going to take a day off on Thursday, Pete, to fish with Dave and my father-in-law. Would you like to join us?"

"I don't fish, Mark. Thought I mentioned that. It bores me to tears. Too bad, too, because this is a fisherman's paradise. Is the boat fixed yet?"

"We're going to rent a boat. I wonder about the gas can, though. Would you know where it is?" He isn't aware of the fingerprint study.

"No. Never had any use for it. We've been prepared for a water rescue for years, but never had need for one. I suppose it's where you left it."

"I'll find it, Pete, thanks. By the way, I'm glad you got the copier fixed."

Donna looks great—rested and in good spirits. "How were the crawfish?" I ask.

"Interesting, but they're more of a tradition than a meal. I squeezed the life out of the little rascals, but still ended up hungry. Dave had to get me a hamburger. The housekeeper was thrilled about the mess in my room. I'm sure the hospital is revising their rules."

"What are you girls up to while Sarah's in school?" I ask Lauren, Millie, and Donna. "We're working on the wedding," Lauren says. "Your absence will be appreciated."

"Lucky thing. Dave, Ace, and I are going to Wal-Mart for fishing gear, and then we're going to plan our trip for tomorrow. You'll be stuck with the convertible, you know."

"We'll suffer," Millie says.

My alarm goes off at 4:00 a.m., waking both of us. Lauren gets up with me to make a pot of coffee. "Why do men do this?" she asks.

"It's the fish that set the agenda."

"Then they deserve to get caught." Lauren is not a pajama person. Before she can slip into her robe, I embrace her and feel her warm body against mine. "It's either fish or me," she says. Reluctantly, I let her go and get dressed.

I wake Dave and call Ace. "I'll bring a donut and some coffee, Ace. We're about to pick you up. Are you ready?"

"For Toledo Bend? You bet!" Every fisherman who takes the sport seriously knows the reputation of Toledo Bend Reservoir. One of the largest man-made bodies of water in the U.S., it's also one of America's top ten bass fishing lakes. Crappie, bream, catfish, and stripers abound as well. Unfortunately, as Lauren and I discovered, the reservoir is treacherous to navigate. The story goes that the 186,000 acres it occupies were to have been cleared before it was filled, but a flood filled it prematurely leaving the trees intact. Boaters have to take care to find clear passages through the treetops. The Sabine River bed is marked with buoys, but getting to the river bed is risky. When the water is at a normal level, the treetops are just submerged. During drier periods they're visible above the water. Either way, they create a great habitat for fish and the risk is worth the reward.

We have a boat gassed up and waiting at a marina on the Texas side of the bridge. Emil has provided a map of the shoreline with an X at lunker heaven. I promise to destroy the map when we're done. The marina sells fresh bait, but Ace and Dave are artificial bait advocates. I'm not so choosy. I've packed two containers of night crawlers. We carry our meager supply of gear, cups of hot coffee, and lunch bags to the boat, toss the PFD's out of the way and shove off. "Who's going to captain this thing?" Dave volunteers so everybody relocates. I move to the bow to man the trolling motor. Ace takes the bench in the middle.

"This is a good boat," Ace says. A sixteen foot, semi-vee boat with a welded aluminum hull, forty horse power outboard, and bow-mounted trolling motor, it has just what we need. Oars are in their locks, if necessary. Dave switches the motor to neutral, squeezes the pump on the gas line, pulls the choke and the rope, and nothing happens. On the third pull, the motor coughs and smokes, then settles down. It sputters until Dave pushes the choke in and switches to reverse. Rigged and ready, we move out of the slip into the morning fog.

"Can you see where you're going?" Ace asks.

"Barely," Dave replies, "I'm going to creep along until the sun is up, and then we can follow the map." We cast plastic worms along the shoreline and immediately hit pay dirt. Before lunch we have our limit. We're going to have a fish dinner.

"There's a place in Hemphill called the Cellar Saloon. We won't have another chance to toast Ace's surrender before the wedding, right?" I ask. All heads nod.

We dock the boat, tip the boy who ices the fish and carries our gear, and then head west to Hemphill. "How is it you know about the Cellar Saloon, Mark?" Ace asks.

"Word gets out, Ace."

"I'm going to go with you to the saloon, but I don't drink alcohol. Stopped a long time ago. I'll be your D.D., okay?"

"No problem," Dave says. "I'll drink yours."

The Cellar Saloon is just that—a basement tavern. The building is probably a century old. Names painted on the side suggest that it has been a dry goods store and a feed store. A worn awning bears the name of the current establishment. We descend three steps to the door and are informed by a small hand-written card that checks will not be honored. I stoop beneath a low doorway and enter a room no brighter than Toledo Bend at 5:30 in the morning. To my right and toward the rear is a short bar with four stools on the straightaway and one around the bend. To my left are several booths. Three tables stand in the center of the room. We're the only customers. "Bar, tables, or booth?" asks a man emerging from the rear. He's tying an apron around a size 48 waist. We opt for a booth. "You're between lunch and dinner, but I can serve you something from the bar."

Dave and I order beer. Ace orders ginger ale. The proprietor brings two buckets, one empty and the other filled with unshelled peanuts. Next, he brings our drinks.

"Interesting place," Dave says. "Hope his rent is reasonable."

"Probably gets a local crowd in the evenings," Ace says.

"Not a sports bar," I note, seeing no television screens. "Anyway, here's to you and Millie, Ace. How do you feel about giving up your freedom?"

"To tell you the truth, knowing Millie is like owning a diamond. Every day she reveals a new facet about herself that never fails to amaze me. We're on in years, but we're looking forward to enjoying our lives together." At that, we raise our glasses and toast their happiness. In fact, we toast their happiness for two and a half hours.

As we rise to leave, the proprietor approaches the table. "Gentlemen, I couldn't help overhearing your conversation." Looking at Ace, he says, "I'd like to propose a toast. May I bring you a drink on the house?"

"As long as it doesn't contain alcohol," Ace says. The man disappears and returns with three glasses. He gives Ace ginger ale, and hands the other glasses to Dave and me. We raise them a bit unsteadily as the bartender makes a final toast.

"What's this?" Dave asks, beating me to the question.

"It's the best I've got from my local stock."

"Local stock of what?" I ask.

"Panther's Breath. Enjoy it, gentlemen." He returns to the bar.

Dave takes a sip of Panther's Breath and sets it down. I finish my drink and wish I hadn't. Ace stops the car twice on the way home to let me heave on the shoulder of the road.

"You're going straight to bed," Lauren says as I stumble into the apartment. I can feel everyone's eyes on me, but Lauren rushes me into the bedroom, undresses me and tucks me in. I dry-heave until I'm exhausted. Finally, I sleep for a few hours. When I get up I feel as though my head is in a vice. Nothing helps. "Aren't you ashamed of yourself?" Lauren scolds.

"Not really," I mumble. "Dave and I had three beers over a couple of hours, not enough to have this effect. It was the Panther's Breath."

"The what?"

"A drink the barkeeper brought to the table. Dave sipped it and I drank it."

"And you got sick."

"Yep. I never tasted anything quite like it, very strong, clear like Vodka. Had a slight head on it. Hit me like a ton of bricks."

"What is it?"

"I intend to find out."

My head is a detonator on Friday morning and the apartment is a mine field with everyone getting ready for the rehearsal. Donna is at the kitchen table going over her wedding address. Dave is loading a stool into the Excursion. Ace is printing handouts on my printer. Sarah is on her cell phone. Lauren and Millie are in the living room working on Millie's dress. Unshaved, droopy-eyed, and stinking, I feel my way into the kitchen where dirty breakfast dishes are exploding in the dishwasher. I'm on my own for breakfast—a just punishment. Still recovering from the events of the previous day, I eat light—juice and a granola bar. I carry a cup of coffee from heaven into the living room and get yelled back into the kitchen. "I don't want coffee spilled on this dress, Mark," Lauren scolds at a volume that could wilt the wedding flowers.

Ace comes into the kitchen with his wedding handouts. "Are you done on the computer?" I ask.

"Yep." I take my coffee into the computer alcove and search "Panther's Breath." Skipping through articles about panthers, pumas, cougars, and breathing, I find what I want: "Names for illegal untaxed liquor include white lightning, rotgut, skull cracker, happy Sally, stump, Panther's Breath, but most often moonshine …" Moonshine I recognize. I've been served an illegal liquor called Panther's Breath at the Cellar Saloon. I search for Dave. He's next to me in the kitchen helping Ace fold the handouts.

"You know what I drank last night?"

"I know you drank too much of it, whatever it was."

"No, actually, I didn't. I've had three beers over a few hours many times, Dave. You know that. We used to share a six-pack watching the Patriots, remember?"

"Yes, I do. Was it the Panther's Breath that made you sick?"

"Exactly. Did you know that Panther's Breath is another name for moonshine?"

"You're kidding. I should have tried some. In New Hampshire they called it Tiger's Sweat."

"Be glad you didn't."

CHAPTER 11

▼

"What's the agenda for today, Mark?" Dave asks.

"The rehearsal is scheduled for 5:00 p.m. and I have dinner reservations at the Mariners Restaurant at 6:30."

Ace, Millie, Lauren, and Donna drive to the church in the convertible. Dave, Sarah, and I go in the Excursion. "Did you take care of the cans?" I ask Sarah.

"Yes."

"Where are they?"

"Under my bed."

"Thanks. Who's helping you with the refreshments after the wedding?"

"Two kids from the youth group and Lonnie."

"Is Lonnie part of the youth group?"

"Not yet."

Perched on her stool at the front of the sanctuary, Donna starts the rehearsal with a prayer, and then puts the wedding party through their paces, including walking through the processional and recessional. It's decided to use recorded music instead of an organist. Red, a boy in the youth group aptly named for his ginger mullet, volunteers to serve as sound technician. At the conclusion Donna gives her usual "get a good night's sleep" lecture and assures everyone that the wedding will be a splendid event. I'm expecting someone to cry, but no one does. These are veterans, after all.

Lauren gives Sarah permission to invite Lonnie to the rehearsal dinner. Sixteen, slightly taller than Sarah, and quiet by nature, Lonnie has become Sarah's friend. As their friendship grows she speaks less about the boy back home. "How's soccer going?" I ask Lonnie, a star player.

"Pretty good. We won this afternoon."

"You played today?"

"Yes sir."

"I'm glad you could join Sarah for dinner." As the others are getting seated in the main dining room, Sarah and Lonnie walk to the deck overlooking Sibley Lake. The setting sun creates a photo-perfect picture. I can see that they're holding hands, so I elbow Lauren and nod toward the window. She looks without expression. I shrug. "I'll call them to the table." From the door I catch Sarah's gaze and beckon them inside.

Dinner is delightful and well served. The evening ends in the Cove Lounge where a one-man band plays a limited repertoire of music for diners and dancers. With a lot of persuasion and a large tip I convince him to play something slow. Ace leads Millie to the postage-stamp dance floor and they sway to the music, Millie leaning heavily on Ace. When the piece ends, I demonstrate my two-step with Lauren, then Sarah, trying not to cripple my ladies. Dave holds Donna's hand at the table until Lauren swaps me for Dave.

Table talk includes the fishing trip of the previous day. "At least I didn't have to clean the fish," I say.

"It's the scourge of the D.D., I guess," Ace says. "You guys would have cut yourselves to ribbons. Besides, you got to try the Panther's Breath."

"What's Panther's Breath?" Sarah asks, turning first to me, then to Lonnie. Lonnie shakes his head and looks at me.

"It's an alcoholic drink that's sold under the table. Some people call it moonshine."

Ace and Millie spend Saturday morning packing for their New Orleans honeymoon. By noon, the Mustang is ready to go, except for Sarah's surprise.

At two o'clock, a FedEx delivery truck pulls into the driveway. The driver knocks at the kitchen door with a long box in his hands. I answer and receive the package, thinking that it's a bit heavy for long-stemmed roses. Addressed to Rev. Donna Kraft, I hand it over. "It's for you," I say, as I set the package on the kitchen table. Donna knows immediately what it is.

"It's Karen! It's Karen!" She carries the package to Sarah's room and closes the door. In less than a minute she strolls down the hallway as if it were a runway, strutting her stuff on her repaired leg, to the applause of her audience. "It's perfect," she says, hugging Dave.

At five minutes before five o'clock, Donna takes her position in the front of the sanctuary wearing a black pants suit under a white alb. Her stole is green for the Pentecost season and her cincture matches her alb. In her hands are her notebook and a copy of the service folder. The wedding party waits in the rear of the sanctuary. The only guests in the pews are Dave, Sarah, Pete, two members of the Lutheran youth group, and Lonnie. They're turned toward the rear of the church. Red is playing a recorded prelude on a CD player in the choir balcony. On my signal he fades the prelude and begins Canon in D by Pachelbel. Lauren, Ace's "best man" leads Ace to the front of the church and they take positions to the left of Donna. When they're ready, Red let's Canon in D play out, then hikes the volume and starts the Wedding March by Lohengrin. Millie is resplendent in her lavender dress. I've seen her dressed up before, but I've never seen her so lovely or so happy. Before we start down the aisle, she plants a kiss on my cheek. I have tears in my eyes as I prepare to give away my friend, the person who once saved my life. Sarah has Millie's cane at the front of the church, so Millie leans on my arm. We walk slowly up the aisle and stop a yard in front of Donna. "Who gives this woman to be married to this man?" Donna asks.

"I do," I say.

Ace comes to Millie's right side and escorts his bride-to-be the rest of the way to the altar. I recede and join the others in the pew. Sarah hands Millie her cane and joins Lonnie as Donna begins the wedding liturgy. The service is brief. Donna's message is perfect, reminding Ace and Millie that they have invited Jesus to be a full partner in their marriage, and that their love for one another should reflect the same love and sacrifice that Jesus demonstrated for his bride, the church. At the right time, Donna announces to the rest of us that "having shared their vows and rings, they are now man and wife." With Donna's permission, Ace places his hands on Millie's cheeks and leans down to give her a respectable peck on the mouth. She pulls away from him, leans her cane against the communion railing, throws her arms around the astonished man, and gives him a real kiss. Everyone laughs out loud.

Right on cue, Red plays Mendelssohn's Wedding March, and the bride and groom recess down the center aisle. Sarah, Lonnie, and her youth group partners slip out before the recession, ostensibly to plug in the coffee pot. Ace and Millie stand at the rear door of the sanctuary and receive the rest of us with a hug or a handshake. Lauren has prepared finger sandwiches and a veggie tray, and Sarah's team has set up a dining area. A few presents are opened before Ace and Millie depart in their convertible for New Orleans, dragging Sarah's string of empty cans behind them.

"Are you happy for your grandfather?" Lauren asks Sarah as we drive back to the apartment.

"Of course I am. Why would you ask that, Mom?"

"Sometimes it's difficult to share love."

"Grandpa and I talked today, Mom. He told me that I will always be his special girl. I already knew that, but it was good to hear it. Besides, Millie's a trip. She'll be fun to have in the family. Did you know she gave me a ring?"

"A ring?"

"It's a beautiful ring that her first husband gave her when he proposed. It's not a diamond or anything. She said they couldn't afford anything like that, but it has a pretty blue stone. She said her eyes were blue once and that's why he gave her the blue stone."

"I wonder why she didn't mention it."

"She did—to me. She said it was special, just for me, and that I should always remember her when I wear it. I really like Millie, Mom, and I'm glad they got married." Lauren squeezes my hand.

CHAPTER 12

▼

The wedding was a needed break from the investigation, but now I need to get back on task. Donna passed a barn while being transported from the Caroline Dormon Trail. She saw activity there which she took to be renovation. Pete seems to know little about the barn.

"I'll need the Excursion today, Mark," Lauren calls from the kitchen. "Have to pick Sarah up at school and take her to ballet."

"Okay. I'll ride my bike to the office and use the service car." Two vehicles are provided for the Natchitoches office of the Forest Service. Pete uses one as his personal vehicle, a practice that's frowned on, but common in the service. The other is available to me and the volunteers. I lock my bike outside the office and go in to get the key. Pete's door is open so I wave to him on my way to the key box.

"What's up, Mark?"

"Going to take the car today, Pete. Lauren's using the Excursion."

"No problem. Help yourself."

"Thought I'd stop by the barn and ask a few questions."

"The barn?"

"Yes, I mentioned that Donna passed a barn on the Dormon Trail service road. Thought I'd see if anyone there has information that could help my investigation."

Pete steps out of his office. "We have a problem, Mark."

"Oh?"

"The car's going in for brake work today. Should have it back by tomorrow. Anything else you can do that doesn't require transportation?" I wait for him to offer the other car, but he says nothing.

"Yes, in fact there is. I plan to speak with the sheriff of Natchitoches Parish."

"On to something?"

"Yes, Sheriff Hardman told me that the Natchitoches Parish sheriff is having problems with rum-running. I'm convinced that alcohol plays a role in my investigations. I had a first-hand experience in Hemphill on Thursday afternoon. The barkeep served moonshine, called it Panther's Breath. I want to get some answers." Pete returns to his office. Before I can say goodbye he has the phone in his hand.

The sheriff's office is on Church Street, a short bike ride from the Forest Service office. I'm cordially greeted and asked to have a seat. The sheriff has just left the office, but should be back shortly. I pick up a magazine and wait. After an hour, I excuse myself and say that I'll call for an appointment. The receptionist apologizes, takes my name, and promises that the sheriff will call.

The ballet studio isn't out of my way, so I stop to see whether Sarah's there. She isn't, so I bike home. "I stopped to see Sarah dance today, but she wasn't there. I thought you were going to pick her up?"

Lauren turns and gives me a puzzled look. "What do you mean she wasn't there? I dropped her off an hour and a half ago. I was just getting ready to pick her up."

"Maybe she got a ride from someone."

"Who?" Lauren asks, reaching for the phone. Sarah's gotten a ride and should be home any minute, the instructor tells her.

"Dave and Donna took the horse buggy tour of Natchitoches this afternoon. They probably stopped by the studio to pick her up."

"Would they do that without calling? I doubt it. Do you know Lonnie's number?" I give her Emil's home phone number. Lettie says that Lonnie hasn't picked anyone up.

"Let's go to the studio." We leave a note for Dave and Donna to call us and head into town. The studio is closed and dark. As we head home, Dave calls. They don't have Sarah and she isn't at the house. We fight a creeping panic. "Let's retrace. You picked Sarah up after school, right?" Lauren nods. "You dropped her off at the studio. It was open and you saw her go in, right?" Another nod. "She knew you were going to pick her up at the end of her hour, right?" Nod. "Has she ever taken a ride with anyone else?" Shake. We pull into the driveway. Dave's rented car is on the street. Lauren rushes into the house.

"Is Sarah here yet?" she asks Donna.

"No. What's going on?"

"Sarah wasn't at the ballet studio when we went to pick her up. They say she got a ride."

"From who?"

"We thought it might have been you."

"Nope. We don't even know where the studio is."

"We went back, but no one was there. I'm going to call the instructor." No answer.

"Do you know any of the other students?"

"Not by their full names."

"We need to call the sheriff's office," I say.

"I thought you said you were taking me home," Sarah says. "This isn't the way to my apartment. You're going the wrong way."

"You're not going home, little girl," the driver sneers.

"Where are we going?"

"Shut up. If you don't stop asking questions, you're going to make us mad, and you really don't want to make us mad. I'm going to stop for something. Behave yourself. The doors are locked and the windows are tinted. You can't get out and no one can see you."

"What's that stuff?" the man in the back seat asks when the driver returns.

"Master's Pride."

"I thought you were my father's friends," Sarah says.

"No questions, remember?" the man in back says as he hits Sarah in the face with his fist.

Sarah's head snaps back and bangs against the window. "What was that for? You can't do this. My father's a ranger. He'll find me."

"That's enough," the driver says as he slams on the brakes.

"Hold still," the other man says while strapping Sarah's ankles and wrists. He hits her again in the face.

"That hurt. My cheek's cut and I'm bleeding in my mouth."

"Listen, we know who your father is, and if he'd minded his own business you wouldn't be taking a ride with us. Now shut your trap or we'll shut it permanently, DO YOU UNDERSTAND?"

The driver turns to the other man, "You shut your mouth, DO YOU UNDERSTAND?"

"Where are we now?" Sarah asks.

"She can see too much," the driver says. "Tape her."

"All I've got is this duct tape."

"Wrap it around her head. Cover her eyes."

"You're pulling out my hair," Sarah complains as her world goes dark.

Twenty minutes after our call, a sheriff's deputy is standing at the kitchen door. He identifies himself and is invited in. "I understand you have a missing daughter, is that right?"

"She didn't come home after ballet lessons," I say.

"How long ago was that?"

"She should have been here about an hour ago."

"Can we sit at the table so I can make out a report?"

"Of course." Lauren sits next to me, facing the deputy. Dave and Donna stand, leaning on the counter. The deputy places a clipboard on the table and begins to write.

"Is this necessary, deputy?" Lauren asks. "Shouldn't we be looking for Sarah instead of making reports?" The moment she asks the question, she realizes how silly it sounds. "I'm sorry. I know the routine. What do you need?" We give him Sarah's particulars and the information he requests.

"Does your daughter have friends in Natchitoches?"

"Of course," Lauren answers.

"Would it be unusual for her to take a ride with her friends?"

"Not necessarily, but she would call us first, especially if she were waiting for us to pick her up."

"Technically, we can't consider Sarah a missing person when she's been missing for less than two hours. It's very possible that she's perfectly safe and will come home with an explanation. In any regard, we'll put the word out to be on the lookout for Sarah."

"When will you pull out all the stops?" I ask.

"If she's not home by bedtime."

"What can we do in the meantime?" Lauren asks.

"I'd suggest that you contact everyone who was at the ballet studio."

We divide the task. Lauren gets the program from the studio's first recital which lists all the students. Dave drives to the instructor's home while Lauren and I contact the students. Donna drives the Excursion through downtown Natchitoches looking for Sarah. We agree to regroup with the deputy at nine o'clock to compare notes. If anyone makes contact with Sarah, they are to summon the troops.

There were eleven students at the first recital. Nine were at the lesson with Sarah. Only one saw Sarah leave. She says that Sarah was standing outside the studio on the sidewalk, as if waiting for her ride.

The instructor's husband sends Dave to the grocery store where his wife is shopping. She saw Sarah get into a car with two young men and thought nothing of it. Everything seemed to be normal. She didn't recognize the young men, but Sarah wasn't resisting in any way. I report the instructor's information to the deputy. "Please make sure that someone is at home at all times," he says, "she might make contact." He doesn't say she might come home.

Donna is the last to check in. She hasn't seen Sarah in town.

"My face hurts and I have to go to the bathroom," Sarah says.

"Don't pee in your pants. We're almost there," the driver says, slowing the car. "We're going to walk for awhile. Let her out and keep her on her feet."

"Get up," the man in the back seat says as Sarah falls out of the car.

"I can't walk with my feet tied."

"I'm going to cut the straps."

"My hands are numb," Sarah says as the blood rushes back into her limbs. "I have to go to the bathroom," Sarah repeats, provoking the men to laughter.

"That's where you're headed," the second man says. "Watch your step. We're in the woods."

"Shut up. Get the sack and the bottle out of the car," the driver says to the second man. "Now, take off your clothes," he says to Sarah.

"No," Sarah replies.

"That was the wrong thing to say," he says, punching her hard in the chest and tearing off her blouse.

"Hey, nice," the other man says as he returns, looking at Sarah's naked body. "Let's have some fun."

"Touch her and you'll deal with me," the driver says. "You know what we were told. Damn, she's peeing on herself." The driver places his foot on Sarah's back and kicks her through the door, then leaves a bag and bottle inside.

"No," Sarah yells as she plunges forward banging her head against a wall.

"Don't talk to me about jurisdictions, Emil. Sarah is my daughter. You kept me at arm's length when she nearly died in an alcoholic coma, but I'm going to be very involved in finding my daughter—believe that."

"Slow down, Mark," Pete says. "This is a civilian matter better left to the sheriff's people. Emil can help. You're too close to it to be objective. You'll be needed at home, I'm sure."

"Whose side are you on, Pete?"

"This isn't a matter of sides, Mark. The Forest Service is not involved in this and has no authority outside of the Kisatchie. If the sheriff asks for our help, we'll oblige, but as of now it's his ball game."

"On behalf of the sheriff's office, I'm asking for everyone's help. If Ranger Garrison wants to be involved, we'll set some ground rules. That goes for Ranger Kraft as well. We're not territorial, Ranger Toussant, and we're not overstaffed. Now I'd suggest that we concentrate on strategy instead of protocol." The deputy assigned to head the case for the Natchitoches Parish sheriff's office is Hervé Durand, a no-nonsense lawman. Born and raised in Natchitoches, he's a widower with two sons in high school. He understands my dilemma.

The meeting is in Pete's office. Pete, Dave, and I are there from the Forest Service. Durand represents the sheriff, and Emil represents the small town of Roberval. His presence is the hardest to understand, but since he's involved in the investigation of the death of Beth Beckett, Pete includes him. Emil, too, has a son in high school. To me, that's important. Pete's clinical approach to the issue is undoubtedly impoverished by not having children.

"Deputy, you're in charge of this investigation. Rangers Garrison and Kraft are at your disposal; however, they're working on a homicide investigation that's growing cold by the minute so we'll be sharing their time."

"At the present, we'll be doing grunt work—interviews, search teams, etc. How many volunteers can you muster for search teams?"

"We have twenty-three volunteers working the Kisatchie Ranger District. Our busy season is just getting underway, but I'll call in the reserve volunteers. That would mean about fifteen."

"I'll take care of organizing teams for the towns outside the Kisatchie," Durand says. "Ranger Kraft, do you know the Kisatchie well enough to head up a search group?"

"No, I'm a visitor here, but I can assist Ranger Garrison, if he's willing."

"Okay, Kraft and Garrison, you get Toussant's team together and get started combing the Kisatchie. I'll meet with the sheriff and get our teams going. Lachine, keep your ears open in Roberval. Everyone report to me not later than 5:00 p.m. each day until we have the girl or call off the search, yes?"

Pete instructs his clerk to round up as many unassigned volunteers and reserves as possible and have them report to the Ranger office at noon. Dave and

I lay out maps of the Kisatchie and Pete divides up the area for the search teams. We agree to return to the office at noon.

"We've done this before, Mark, remember?" Dave says on the drive to the apartment.

"You mean on the Appalachian Trail?"

"Sure. And we found our man, didn't we?"

"Wayne Clark."

"Yep. And we'll find Sarah, too."

Donna and Lauren are drinking coffee at the kitchen table. Lauren's red-eyed and tired. The instructor from the ballet school has just left. "She's really upset," Donna says.

"Did she have any more information?" Dave asks.

"No, but she was able to describe the car to the sheriff's deputy. I don't know how much help it'll be since she didn't know the year or make, just that it was an older, blue four-door sedan. She said the young men were wearing what she called 'sloppy clothes.'"

"That could describe anyone these days," Dave says. "Did she give any description of the men?"

"White, probably teens, baseball-type caps turned backwards, bouncy."

"Bouncy?"

"Like bouncing to rap music."

"Were they wearing headphones?"

"I asked the same thing. She didn't think so."

"High, possibly? Or drunk?"

"Sarah wouldn't have left with them in that case."

"She left voluntarily?"

"Seems so."

"Honey, Mark and I have to be in Pete's office at noon. We're going to head up search teams at the Kisatchie while Deputy Durand organizes search teams in the surrounding areas. Will you stay with Lauren?"

"Of course, Dave."

"I'm going to get into uniform," I tell Dave and Donna. Lauren follows me into the bedroom. As soon as I close the door, she collapses in my arms in tears.

"Something's terribly wrong, Mark. Why would anyone do this?"

"We'll know in time, but for now we have to keep it together, Lauren—for Sarah's sake."

"Don't even begin to tell me how to act, Mark. This is my only child—my flesh and blood. If I want to go to pieces, that's just what I'll do."

"I'm sorry. You're right, but I can't be in two places at once—holding your hand and finding Sarah. You have to tell me what you want me to do."

"No, I'm sorry, Mark. I love you. Please understand. You have to find Sarah. I'll be okay with Donna. I'm even thinking of calling Daddy." She has never called Ace "Daddy" to me before. "They'd never forgive me if they found out that we didn't call them as soon as Sarah disappeared."

"You're right. Do you want me to call them?"

"I have their agenda. Let me get myself together, and then I'll call."

"Did you call your Dad?" I ask Lauren on my third call for an update. I keep hoping that Sarah will have called or come home.

"I didn't have to, Mark. They called first. I didn't even let Daddy tell me about their trip. I just interrupted him, and then cried into the phone."

"I'm sure he understood, Lauren."

"They're checking out of the hotel and coming back here. They'll come to the apartment as soon as they get to Natchitoches. They can stay in Sarah's room until she gets back, if …"

"Don't finish the sentence. There's no 'if.' She'll be home."

"You don't know that, Mark, and neither do I. We both know the rule of thumb—the longer it takes the less chance of a good outcome. We've been in law enforcement long enough not to kid ourselves, Mark."

"We have to keep hope alive, Lauren."

"I love you, Mark. I need you more than ever."

"Should I come home?"

"No, I'll be okay."

The gathering point for the Forest Service volunteers is the Longleaf Vista Recreation Area. Pete has drawn search maps for Dave and me. Dave, who is completely unfamiliar with the Kisatchie District, is to take his team along trails and Forest Service roads north of the Scenic Byway. I'm to take my team along trails and FS roads south of the Byway. Because there is no mobile phone service in the Kisatchie, search leaders are given battery-powered radio sets to keep in touch. Our volunteers are mostly older folks, so hiking through the wilderness is ruled out.

Pete has also contacted two groups that regularly use the Kisatchie: a group called the Equine Explorers will begin a horseback search, and an ATV club will begin a 4-wheel search of the wilderness areas. Pete will lead the riders and Emil will lead the drivers. They are to assemble at the Kisatchie Bayou Recreation Area. The plan seems workable.

By one o'clock Dave and I are ready to go. We leave one volunteer at the starting point to direct latecomers. Dave has six volunteers and I have seven. A vehicle with emergency supplies and water will follow each group. The plan is to cover twenty feet on each side of the trails or roads looking for Sarah or anything that might be evidence of her presence. Dave and I will be the only searchers to call out for Sarah so that we can hear a response. We gather all of the searchers in a circle and Dave offers a prayer for a successful outcome. We'll search until sundown, then resume at sunrise each day until the Kisatchie work is done.

I radio Pete to let him know that we're engaged. He reports that the equine group has already been dispatched and Emil is about to leave with the ATV's. The search is on in the Kisatchie. I wonder how Deputy Durand is doing on the civilian front. I'm not comfortable being out of contact with the home front, but there's no public phone in the Kisatchie District where I can call Lauren. It'll have to wait until we end the search at sundown.

CHAPTER 13

▼

"My head hurts," Sarah says as she tenderly peels the remaining duct tape from her hair and swollen face. Awakened by sunlight beaming from a vent near the top of the cathedral ceiling, Sarah gets her first glimpse of her jail—a glorified outhouse with a toilet that sits over a hole in the ground. The vent is too high to reach and too narrow to crawl through. No sink or mirror. "I wonder if they've locked the door," she thinks, surprised to discover that the latch moves. The door, however, does not.

A bag of Master's Pride and a gallon bottle of clear liquid have been thrown inside the door. "It's dog food," Sarah thinks, after opening and closing the Master's Pride. Thirsty, she removes the cap from the bottle and smells the contents. It's the same stuff she drank at school. Swollen, cracked lips notwithstanding, she returns the cap to the bottle.

"My parents must be going crazy. I have to get out of this place, but how? Surely, if the men wanted to kill me they could have. Why leave me here? For how long? Will anyone hear me if I scream? Are the men still outside? I'll scream anyway." No response. "I'll scream again." Still nothing.

"I told you to stay put. When I call I want you to be there, do you understand? I won't call twice again."

"I understand. I was making a delivery."

"I don't give a damn what you were doing. You follow orders. How did it go last night?"

"Just as you said—she's in the shithouse at Red Bluff."

"Was Red Bluff closed?"

"Yeah, just like you said."

"How did it go at the dance school?"

"She believed it when we told her we were friends of her old man. She got right in the car, but we had to pop her a few times to keep her quiet."

"How bad was she hurt?"

"A few bruises maybe."

"Did you leave her something to eat?"

"Sure, like you said," chuckling.

"What's so funny?"

"We left her a bag of dog food and a bottle of Panther's Breath."

"You idiots! I told you to leave food and water." Silence. "Did you hear me?"

"I heard. What do you want us to do?"

"Nothing, I'll take care of it. If anything happens to her, you two are in trouble. I want her to stay alive. Now, get back to your deliveries and keep your mouths shut, understand?"

"Yes sir," the driver said, raising his middle finger at the phone.

We call the search at seven, return to the Longleaf Vista Recreation Area, and dismiss the searchers with instructions to return at six a.m. Neither Pete nor Emil has information about Sarah. They will also resume searching in the morning.

"Let's download on the way to your apartment," Dave says. "I don't know if I've worked with a better group. I don't believe we missed anything, Mark. We should wrap up our area sometime tomorrow."

"Same here, Dave, but I'm worried that the park visitors will disturb evidence. There's not much we can do."

"Looks like Ace and Millie are back," Dave says as we park behind their convertible. The mood is solemn in the apartment.

"Sarah will need her room," Millie says. "We'll get a room in the Holiday Inn Express." Her confidence, meant well, fails to rally the group.

"A reporter was here from the Shreveport Times," Donna says. "The news about Sarah will be on TV tonight and in the Times tomorrow. Lauren gave them a picture of Sarah, and they have all the information they need, so we told them we don't want any interviews."

"What's the plan for tomorrow, Mark?" Millie asks.

"We didn't find anything helpful today, so we're planning to resume our search at daybreak, and then we'll regroup at five o'clock."

"Millie and I will post pictures of Sarah around town," Donna says.

Conversation stops when Sarah's name is mentioned on television. A picture showing Sarah standing next to the Excursion and an appeal to anyone with information is followed by a graphic displaying the phone numbers to call.

"If people give this stuff to their dogs, it must be safe," Sarah thinks. Gagging on the dry kibbles, she reaches for the gallon bottle and drinks a swallow of Panther's Breath. "Ugh," she mutters, spitting it out of her mouth, "this stuff is awful."

"Help me," she screams through the air vent, but there's no response. She retreats to the corner of her prison as the sunlight gives way to darkness.

"I stink," she thinks to herself. "The toilet doesn't flush, and this whole place is starting to stink." Startled by a loud thump and shuffling footsteps on the roof, she freezes. "Someone's walking on the roof." The footsteps stop, followed by a dull thud on the ground outside the air vent and a low growl and hissing. Sarah jumps to her feet at the sound of scratching outside the wall where she's sitting. The scratching pauses, then resumes outside the door. She hears sniffing at the crack beneath the door. "Whatever it is, it knows I'm here." The visitor retreats, and after an hour of intense listening, Sarah stretches out on the cool floor and sleeps.

Awakened by another sound at the door, Sarah scoots to the farthest wall. The door opens slowly and a beam of a bright light searches the room. "Stay where you are and turn so I can see you," a male voice says.

"Please don't hurt me. Please let me out of here."

"You're not going anywhere yet, Sarah. Just turn your face so I can see you."

"I'm naked."

"I just want to see your face." She covers herself with her hands and turns toward the intense light, squinting in its glare.

"I'm leaving some supplies and clothes for you, Sarah. The water's not for drinking. Use it to clean yourself. Drink what's in the bottle if you get thirsty. It won't kill you."

"There's a bear or something outside. I'm afraid."

"There aren't bears around here, Sarah. It's probably a puma. He can't get in and you can't get out." The door is slammed shut. She hears two men arguing outside, but can't make out what they're saying. Both voices are familiar. Sarah lays awake until the sun shines through the vent.

Curious and ravenous, Sarah empties the plastic bag left during the night. It contains six grain bars, a bunch of bananas, a roll of paper towels, and an unmarked gallon bottle of clear liquid—the same kind of bottle containing the alcohol. She removes the cap and sniffs—water. She splashes some on her face, being careful not to get any in her mouth. In a second bag are the things she had when she was abducted. The blouse is torn and the clothes are wrinkled, but she's grateful for them.

Cleaner and covered, she inhales a grain bar and banana, then, with renewed energy, determines to get out of her prison.

When we assemble for the search, I'm pleased to see that the crew has recruited friends and neighbors for the day's work. Dave resumes his search north of the byway with thirteen, and I proceed south with twelve. The search should move faster today. We have no contact with Pete and Emil before we leave. They have to assemble horses and ATV's before resuming the search in their areas.

Millie and Donna are already on the street when we leave the apartment. Ace is staying home with Lauren. Deputy Durand has over thirty volunteers from community groups searching the rural areas around Natchitoches. The Louisiana State Police are stopping older blue sedans in the Parish. The media are making appeals. If Sarah's in the area, she'll be found. If ...

At two o'clock my team has completed searching the assigned areas and is ready to assist Dave's group. By three o'clock the trails and FS roads on both sides of the Scenic Byway have been combed. The volunteers on foot are not suited for rougher terrain, so I call the search complete. So far, none of the teams has found Sarah or evidence pointing to her whereabouts.

Deputy Durand arranges a table in the parish administration building for the five o'clock meeting. Present are Emil and Lonnie, Pete, Dave, Durand, and me. We sit at the discussion table. A clerk and two visitors from the Louisiana State Police sit near Deputy Durand. No one from the media is invited, although several reporters are in the waiting area outside the conference room.

Durand opens the meeting with a summary of his activities. "With the help of scores of volunteers and some troopers we've scoured the area outside the Kisatchie and come up empty. No older blue sedans similar to the one witnessed at the scene of the reported abduction have been located. Without a tag number or make of automobile, it's questionable whether we'll identify the car.

"I have another concern. The sheriff just informed me that the missing girl was cited recently for underage drinking in an incident at the middle school. It's possible that her drinking behavior has some bearing on her disappearance. As a result, we've alerted liquor stores and alcohol licensees to be on the lookout for her."

"Hold on," I say. "As most of you know, Sarah is my step-daughter. She does not have a drinking problem. She got into a forced situation at the school and almost died from alcohol poisoning."

Dave puts his hand on my arm and says softly, "You're making it worse, Mark. Let it go."

Pete asks for a recess and leads me outside the conference room. "I asked you to stay out of this investigation, Ranger. Now I'm ordering you off the case. I'll have Dave drive you home."

"Yes sir," I say. I'm furious.

"Come on, Mark," Dave says. "Our work in the Kisatchie is done. Sarah's not there. We need to let Durand and the troopers do their work. We're too closely involved. Remember Wayne Clark, Mark. You didn't let go of that one, either, and it almost cost you your life."

CHAPTER 14

▼

On the way to the apartment my cell phone rings, but no one responds when I answer. Assuming that it's a computer-generated call, I'm about to hang up when a muffled voice says, "Ranger Garrison, listen carefully. Pack your things, go home, and your daughter will be released." Before I can respond, the caller hangs up.

"Could you hear that?" I ask Dave.

"No."

"Someone told me to go home and Sarah would be released."

"Did you recognize the voice?"

"It was disguised, muffled."

"This has to do with you. Whose buttons are you pushing?"

"I don't know, but I intend to find out."

"Mark, think carefully about what you say. If you stay on, Sarah may pay for it."

"What would you do?"

"Leave the area. Go back to New England with your whole family."

"And let the homicide investigation go cold?"

"And let Sarah go cold?"

As soon as Dave and I get home I contact the cell phone company for an id on the caller. They tell me I'll need a court order.

"Well, look who's home for dinner—it's the mighty road warrior!"

"What kind of greeting is that, Lettie?"

"What kind do you want, Emil, a welcome wagon reception? You hardly come home for dinner anymore, and where's Lonnie?"

"He's getting the ATV off the truck. He'll be here in a minute."

"Did you find the girl?"

"You'd know it if we did, Lettie. It'd be all over the news."

"Norma said you caught the kidnappers in Roberval."

"Who's Norma?"

"Only our neighbor to the rear. If you'd stick around here long enough you might get to know the neighbors."

"What kind of nonsense is she spreading?"

"She said she saw you at the traffic light talking to two men in a blue sedan. Isn't that the kind of car the girl was kidnapped in?"

"She's a busybody. I stopped a car like that, but it didn't have anything to do with the girl. You tell Norma that."

"Thanks, Dad," Lonnie said, slamming the screen door behind him.

"For what, Lonnie? And don't slam the damn door."

"For the dog food."

"You bought dog food for that mutt?" Lettie asked. "Aren't our scraps good enough anymore?"

"Forget it," Emil said.

"Old Boy never had Master's Pride, Dad. Hope it don't spoil him."

"Deputy, we need to talk, now," I say.

"I heard that your boss took you off the case."

"That's his prerogative."

"You're too close to the case, Ranger, and besides, it doesn't appear that the girl, I mean Sarah, is in the Kisatchie."

"I'm not calling about that, Deputy. I got a threatening call on the way home today." I tell him about the call and that I need a court order to find out where the call came from.

"It's not always possible to trace cell phone calls. Some prepaid phones are untraceable, but we can give it a try. I'm sure the judge'll issue an order, and I'll follow up."

"Thanks."

"Ranger, I appreciate all that you and Ranger Kraft have done since Sarah disappeared, but both the sheriff and I agree that you should work with your family in an unofficial capacity. Keep me informed if you come up with anything, okay?"

"You'll let me know where the call came from?"

"If we get lucky, you bet."

Exhausted and weak on her third night, Sarah is awakened by heavy scratching on the door. "Its back," she thinks, remaining still. A growl grows into snarls, then silence. "Whatever it is, it'll probably leave at daybreak."

Standing, she feels dizzy and her lips are cracked from dehydration. For the second day, she hasn't urinated and is desperately thirsty. Approaching the bottles, she decides that the alcohol is safer to drink than the water. Bacteria won't survive in alcohol, so Sarah sips enough to wet her mouth and throat. After a few minutes, she vomits. Even so, she sips more until she falls asleep. On awakening she eats a grain bar and banana and sips more alcohol. With renewed strength, she shouts as loud as possible with her dry throat, but without result.

Sarah looks for something with which to open the door latch. "My toe shoes," she thinks. "Are they in the clothes bag?" Emptying the bag, her pulse quickens. She removes a short shank, about two inches long, from the toe box of one shoe.

"A bathroom door should lock people out, but why would anyone make a bathroom door that would lock people in?" she reasons to herself. She remembers Mark telling her that if she were ever locked into a car trunk or refrigerator she would find a release inside to open the door. "Why wouldn't they make bathroom doors with safety devices to allow anyone to open the door from either side in an emergency? Who would let their kid go into a bathroom that would trap him inside? Someone has rigged this door to keep it from opening."

Durand gets lucky and calls me. "The threatening call came from a prepaid cell phone. Users of prepaid phones provide the phone company personal information that's tightly protected; however, under subpoena or court order, the company's obligated to provide the identity of the user," Durand reports.

"Who was the caller?"

"That's the catch. We know who purchased the prepaid phone, but that person couldn't have placed the call."

"I don't understand."

"The phone belonged to one of two boys who died in a recent auto incident in Texas."

"What is he thinking?" Lauren asks when I tell her that Pete has ordered me off the investigation. "Sarah's our daughter."

"Pete's not in charge of the investigation. He's in charge of me. Durand agrees that I'm too close to this, but he has no problem with us continuing to search for Sarah as her family. It just so happens that three of the people in this apartment are law enforcement officers. You and I are veteran crime fighters, and Dave is a seasoned forest ranger. We can mobilize our own investigation. I suggest that we get started as soon as we can get everyone together and divvy up the work, high five?" Excited, Lauren slaps my hand.

"Mark, I have to ask this. Do you think Sarah's still alive?"

"There's no way of knowing. We have to operate on the assumption that she is." I can't help thinking of Lovely Hampden and Beth Beckett, but I don't share my thoughts with Lauren.

"I don't think we should mention what we're doing to anyone outside the house?"

"Why?"

"I don't know, Mark, but the boat incident, the threatening call, and Sarah's disappearance suggest to me that the person responsible is very close to us." That's one of the things I like about women—they have sharp instincts. Dave has told me many times that women make great preachers because they appeal to the heart as well as the mind. It's the same with policewomen. They have a sensitivity about people that men often lack. I've learned with Judy, and now Lauren, to heed their instincts.

"Tell me more."

"I can't. I haven't been involved in the investigation, but I don't think we're going to have to go far to find Sarah."

"When we do, I think we're also going to solve the murders of Lovely and Beth." As soon as I say it, I wish I hadn't.

"Mark, do you think …"

"It doesn't matter what I think right now, Lauren. Let's stay focused on Sarah. Can you round up your father and Millie, and I'll round up Dave and Donna. Let's have a working lunch in the living room and do what we've done many times—review the facts, Ma'am."

"Like at the Blue Light in New Hampshire?" Lauren asks. I do indeed remember working with Lauren on an investigation in New Hampshire. I discovered personal feelings that came too soon after Judy's death. Lauren understood and gave me time. It's one of the things I love about her.

"We'll have time for that when Sarah's found." She touches my hand and gazes into my eyes.

"I love you, Mark."

"Everything's going to work out, Lauren, you'll see."

Since Dave and I are no longer officially representing the Forest Service and Lauren has no affiliation with a law enforcement agency in this area, and since we're close to Texas, we decide to call ourselves a posse. Dave nominates me to be the unofficial sheriff of the posse.

"We'll have no official status," I say.

"Who can we trust outside the posse?" Lauren asks, still suspicious of the locals.

"Hervé Durand. I think we should keep him informed of our work, for our own protection, and besides, he has two kids in high school."

"None of us has a link to the younger population, the people Sarah might hang out with," Ace says.

"What about Lonnie?" Donna asks. "Can we include him in the posse?"

"I don't think so," Lauren says.

"Let's think this over," I say. "Lonnie cares about Sarah. I've seen them together. There's some chemistry there."

"Emil has been more of a hindrance than a help," Lauren says.

"If we make it clear that our work is low key, Lonnie may cooperate," Dave says.

"Blood's thicker than water," Donna says.

"I say we trust the boy. Hormones speak louder than blood at his age," Millie says.

"Let's take a vote. All who want Lonnie to work with us raise your hand." Lauren's are the only hands down. "It's a done deal—Lonnie's in. I'll fill him in on what we decide today."

The posse settles in the living room. Millie's at one end of the couch, Donna at the other, with Dave in between. Ace brings kitchen chairs for Lauren and me, and then sits in my recliner. I pass out paper and pencils and there's a moment of reshuffling. "Okay," I start, "let's do this logically. First, we pool our knowledge. Second, we make a plan. Third, we make assignments. Any objections? There being none, I'll give an overview."

"Sarah was picked up by two …"

"You can't start there, Mark," Lauren interrupts. "You have to go back to the reason we're here. Think of the threatening phone call. Sarah's disappearance is linked to your investigation."

"Check. We're here because of the Beckett homicide." I fill Ace and Millie in on the deaths of Lovely Hampden and Beth Beckett. "But my investigation has had little support from the locals, including my supervisor, Pierre, and my so-called helper, Emil. Both have handled the homicides like a game of Clue in slow motion. First, the ME's report, a vital part of my investigation, was difficult to pin down. No sooner had my investigation gotten under way when a fringe group at Sarah's middle school tried to recruit her into their drinking group with a mug of liquor, resulting in her hospitalization in an alcoholic coma. When I tried to get to the bottom of that assault I ran up against the principal, Emil, and Pete, all of whom reminded me that I was out of my jurisdiction. Shortly after, the only witness to the event was beaten into silence. Later, one of the fringe group died in an auto accident now considered a probable homicide. Obviously, I was stirring someone's water."

"Don't leave out the fishing trip," Lauren adds.

"Right, I was getting to that. Lauren and I came within a nautical mile of our lives after I started inquiring about Sarah's event." I narrate details about the incident at Toledo Bend, including the drilled holes in the bottom of the boat, the emptied gas can, and the wet return to shore.

"The only people who knew about our fishing trip were Pete and Emil, and the only readable prints on the gas can were theirs and ours. Was this a coincidence?" Lauren asks in an accusing tone.

"I have to admit I was surprised to learn of Pete's prints since he hadn't used the boat, and he tried to dismiss the incident when I reported it to him, suggesting that we were novices at fishing the treacherous Toledo Bend Reservoir."

"Mark, didn't you tell me that you think moonshine is somehow connected with all of this?" Dave asks.

"Moonshine?" Millie asks. "You mean the good old stuff that we get at Woody's in New Hampshire?" She winks at Ace who smiles.

"Something like it, Millie," I say, "but here they call it Panther's Breath."

"Happy panthers, I'll bet," Millie quips.

"Not so happy," I say. "Lovely Hampden and Beth Beckett were drunk when they were killed, possibly even unconscious. Sarah barely recovered from an alcoholic coma. Two boys, at least one of whom was involved in Sarah's incident, were murdered in Texas—both too drunk to drive. The cell phone used to make the threatening call I received was made on one of their phones. Ace, Dave, and I were offered Panther's Breath in Texas to celebrate your marriage, Millie. I was foolish enough to drink it and got very sick. Sheriff Hardman of Caddo Parish told me that we have a problem with rum-running in this area. Now, you tell me—am I off base when I see a common denominator here?"

"How does Sarah's disappearance fit in with all of this?" Ace asks.

"Okay. Until I received the threatening phone call, I wasn't sure. I ruled out a kidnapping for ransom. Anyone who would do that doesn't know what rangers earn. As you know, I was told if I went back to New Hampshire, Sarah would be released. That's a good and bad story. At least we know Sarah's alive, but we don't know where or in what condition. And we don't have a deadline for my return to New Hampshire. Bottom line—we have to move fast to find her. I'm sure that when we do, we'll also solve the homicides. Then, we'll go home to New Hampshire on our own terms."

"Do you mean that, Mark?" Lauren asks.

"You bet I do."

"That's a Reader's Digest account of where we are. Any questions?"

"Yes. What now?" Ace asks.

"Now we make a plan." No sooner have I spoken than Lonnie shows up at the kitchen door.

Sarah notices that when the latch is twisted downward she can see the bolt move into the door. The door should open, but it doesn't. She twists the latch downward and slides the shank from her toe shoe between the bolt and the door to keep the bolt from closing. It's a cloudy day and there's little light in the bathroom, but by placing her head on the floor she can see under the door. Beyond the door is a wall and at the bottom of the wall Sarah can see the end of a board about four inches wide and several inches thick. The board is standing on end and leaning toward her. "This door is blocked," she thinks, "not locked." She tries to shake the board loose by banging on the door, but that loosens the shoe shank allowing the bolt to close, sending the shank out of reach into the crack between the door and the frame. In frustration she sips from the alcohol bottle and sits back against the wall. She likes the way the alcohol helps her relax, so she sips again until her eyes grow heavy.

Once again she's awakened by the animals. Without a watch she doesn't know how long she has slept, but it's very dark. Sarah can't see stars through the vent.

"The animals must smell me." She can smell herself and doesn't like the odor. "The door," she thinks. "They've come to the door every time." She goes to the door and hisses. Immediately, the footsteps on the roof stop and she hears a soft thump outside the vent, then a snarl. Is it really a puma?

The door is the only protection between her and the animal just inches away, but if she gets it stirred up enough, perhaps it'll dislodge the board. She hisses again causing loud snarling and growling. Then she bangs on the door. It's a big mistake. She scares the animal away.

Within thirty minutes it's back—on the roof, outside the vent, at the door. This time it's cautious. A light scratching on the door, then quiet hissing, then a loud growl. Sarah hisses back and the game is on again. She can hear the soft footsteps—are they pawsteps? She thinks of Raunchy, a stray cat that she fed for a month or so before he ran away. Raunchy loved to play tug-of-war with Sarah's socks. Are pumas just big cats? She retrieves a ballet stocking from her bag and rolls it lengthwise pushing the toe end under the door and moving it from side to side. A heavy paw slaps the ground until it makes contact. It wants to play!

The sound of the board falling startles Sarah and the animal, and the night grows silent.

Sarah tries the latch again. Her prison door opens a crack, then slams shut as the full weight of an animal lunges against it. It's still outside. The bolt clicks into place and the door is secured, but no longer braced from the outside. "The men could return," she thinks. "I should leave now, but not with the animal there." She eats a grain bar and banana, takes a sip of alcohol, and waits for what seems an eternity.

As the sun begins to rise, Sarah hears a commotion outside, a shuffling sound and low growling. It continues until daylight, and then everything gets quiet again. She peeks outside and sees the bloody carcass of a spotted fawn lying on the grass about twenty feet from the bathroom. A raccoon sits up and freezes in place as Sarah steps cautiously into the cool grayness of morning and surveys her surroundings.

About one hundred feet from the bathroom, across an open area, she sees a sign reading "Kisatchie National Forest Campground, Red Bluff". She's in Kisatchie! Except for the dead fawn and the escaping raccoon, she's alone. Quickly, she gathers her remaining grain bars, bananas, and paper towels and runs into the forest as fast as her weak muscles will carry her. The bathroom door closes behind her. Catching her breath behind an ancient pine tree, she decides to follow a dirt road from a distance, careful not to be seen until she's safe.

CHAPTER 15

▼

"Hi, Lonnie," Lauren says as the boy steps into the kitchen.

"Any word?" Lonnie asks.

"None yet, Lonnie. Have a seat. I'll be right back." Lauren steps into the living room and gets permission from the posse to invite Lonnie into the living room.

Escorting Lonnie, Lauren says, "I believe you know everyone here. We have something to discuss with you." I bring Lonnie up to speed on what the posse has discussed and invite him to join our effort. He quickly agrees.

"We don't plan to discuss what we're doing, Lonnie, with anyone outside the posse except Deputy Sheriff Durand. Do you understand?" Dave cautions.

"Sure. That's okay. What about my Dad?"

"Even your Dad," Ace says, knowing that it's a delicate matter for Lauren and me.

"I don't understand why we wouldn't discuss it with my Dad," Lonnie says.

"If that's a problem," Ace says, "we understand. You're free to go."

"No. I want to help find Sarah."

"Good. We're just getting ready to decide how we're going to proceed. Can you join us?"

"Sure. I was going to the library. My folks don't expect me back for a few hours."

"Bring a chair from the kitchen, Lonnie, and have a seat," Lauren says.

I continue addressing the posse, "Lauren thinks that Sarah's close by. She's a good cop with good instincts. Since Durand is doing a careful job searching outside the Kisatchie, and since we won't have any interference in the forest, I suggest we resume our search there. Any objections?"

"Lonnie, you were on one of the ATV teams, right?" Dave asks. Lonnie nods. "Mark, I mean Ranger Garrison, and I led the teams on foot. Perhaps you could look at this map and show us the areas that the ATV teams searched." The Kisatchie Ranger District map is spread out on the floor. Lonnie traces the areas searched by his ATV team.

"I can't tell you where the horse teams searched," Lonnie says, "or where my Dad's ATV team searched. Ranger Toussant gave each of us a marked map."

"Same with us, Lonnie," I say.

"Your team covered the wooded sections of the area while my walking team searched from the roads, Lonnie," Dave says. "Let's compare notes to see if we covered everything in our zone since the horse teams didn't go into the wildlife preserve." Lonnie gets on his knees and runs his finger across the area that his ATV team searched. Dave watches carefully then does the same, tracing the roads that his walking team searched.

Lonnie says, "We didn't go into the Red Bluff Camp. That area's closed for this summer. They're re-grading the access road. That's probably why it wasn't marked on our map." Dave's head snaps up and his eyes catch mine.

"We didn't go into that area either. It wasn't on our map," Dave says.

"Let's make sure we go back there," I say.

"What about the old barn I saw?" Donna asks. "Did anyone go there?"

"My team searched along the Caroline Dormon Trail," I say, "but I didn't see any barns."

"The barn wasn't on the Dormon Trail," Donna says. "It was on a service road leading back to the Scenic Byway."

"My map didn't cover any of the service roads," I say. "That's another area we need to visit."

"Well, what are we waiting for?" Millie asks. "Time's a wasting."

"Lonnie, you know these areas. Can we get into the Red Bluff Camp on foot? And what about the old barn?"

"Red Bluff is a walk-in tent camping area. No problem getting there, but I don't know about any barn." Everyone turns toward Donna.

"I saw the barn from the service road," she says. "It was about a soccer field off the road. There were a few cars there, but I didn't see any people. Smoke was coming from a chimney on the back side of the roof, so I know that something was going on there."

"Could you find it again?" Dave asks.

"I don't know. I was on an ATV stretcher kind of deal."

"I could take someone on my ATV," Lonnie says.

"Do you have access to an ATV?" I ask.

"Sure, we own one. Or I could borrow one."

"Borrow one," Dave says, "and have it ready to go first thing tomorrow morning, okay?—without discussing it with anyone." Lonnie looks puzzled, but agrees.

"Why tomorrow?" Millie asks. "That means another night for Sarah."

"It's too late to get it done before nightfall," I answer, "and besides, we'll need to prepare. Now, Dave, will you go with Lonnie tomorrow?" Dave nods and glances at Lonnie.

"Lauren and I will search Red Bluff Camp as soon as the sun comes up."

"Are you planning to leave Ace and Donna and me here to twiddle our thumbs?" Millie asks.

"Are you kidding?" I say. "You're going to take the Excursion and pictures of Sarah and ask everyone you encounter whether they've seen her, driving the entire length of the Scenic Byway and visiting all of the camps."

"How will we stay in touch?" Dave asks.

"Deputy Durand provided the radios for the first search," I say. "We'll use those. Ace, please arrange to have them here tomorrow morning." Ace nods.

"All right, everyone. We've got work to do. Let's get busy."

The pine trees provide little cover for someone trying to stay hidden. Their foliage is a hundred feet in the air, each tree competing for a ray of sunlight, but the tall giants have shed their needles for decades, creating a blanket that silences each step. Carefully and quietly, Sarah seeks out the cover of low-hanging magnolias and wild azalea bushes, moving stealthily from bush to bush, unaware that Red Bluff Camp is closed to the public. She moves along the fringe of the dirt road for less than an hour until the road ends at an intersection. A chain is slung across the road. Moving past the chain, Sarah can see that the road to the right is well-rutted, so she follows it for about ten minutes until she hears a motor. Fearing her captors, she collapses to the ground and crawls behind a small holly bush. An ATV moving slowly passes behind a stand of pine trees, obstructing her view. It's headed in the direction of Red Bluff Camp. She remains motionless until it's out if sight, then continues her escape.

"I've got to get something to drink," Sarah says, resting behind the stump of a fallen pine tree. Weak from hunger and thirst, her legs scratched, and her head spinning, Sarah fights to stay alert. A black squirrel startles her as it leaps onto the stump then flees. She eats her last banana and tosses the peel overhead behind her. The peel splashes. Water. Sarah walks toward the sound and finds a small stream tumbling down a short hill over sandy soil. It's as clear as glass. Sitting in the stream, she lets the water run over her legs and feet, then scoops some into her hands, splashes it on her face and lets some run down her throat. It tastes wonderful. She becomes aware of some movement in the woods and remains still. A fawn emerges from behind a clump of azalea bushes and drinks from the stream. The serenity of the moment is broken by the sound of a car.

Sarah pulls on her shoes and sloshes to the crest of a small hill. A shiny black SUV comes into view. She sees emergency lights on the vehicle, but can't read the lettering on the side. Quickly, she runs to the road waving her arms. As the SUV comes closer, she reads the words, "Town of Roberval."

CHAPTER 16

▼

"Hey, listen to this front page article in the Reporter," Lauren says on our way to the Red Bluff Camp, 'FBI Enters Investigation of Auto Accident that Killed Two in Texas. Texas and Louisiana law enforcement agencies have invited the FBI to assist in the investigation of the deaths of two Louisiana teenagers killed in an auto accident on Texas Highway 21. The Sabine County ME has determined by the alcohol content in the blood of the victims that they were in a state of unconsciousness at the time of the crash. It was also determined at the scene that neither was restrained by a safety belt. A traffic reconstructionist testified at the inquest that from the absence of tire marks on the roadway it could be determined that the vehicle was driven to the edge of the roadway, then pushed to the crest of the hill from which it rolled approximately 70 feet into a tree, ejecting one passenger through the windshield and crushing the other. The inquiry resulted in a finding of homicide. The FBI has met with Texas and Louisiana officials and will assist in the identification and arrest of the person or persons responsible. The names of the victims are being withheld.' We already know the identity of one victim. It was one of the group that poisoned Sarah."

"There's the turnoff for Red Bluff," Lauren says as we enter the National Red Dirt Wildlife Management Preserve. I turn off of the Longleaf Trail Scenic Byway and head northwest toward Red Bluff Camp. When I reach the final dirt road leading into the camp, a chain is stretched across the road. "Camp closed for road repair," reads a sign suspended from the chain.

"Got your walking shoes on, Lauren?"

"Yep. Let's go."

I pack water bottles, radio, and map into my daypack and we leave the Excursion on the shoulder of the road. Two hours later, after hiking about six miles on two dirt roads, we see a clearing. A carved sign announces Red Bluff Camp. We've seen no sign of Sarah. We split up and hike on opposite sides of the road, ten feet from the roadbed, hoping to find some evidence of our missing girl.

"Let's check the vault toilet," Lauren suggests.

The black SUV stops at the sight of Sarah and pulls to the side of the dirt road. The windows of the vehicle are tinted, so Sarah can't see inside. The passenger door is opened from inside. Safe at last, Sarah jumps into the vehicle and is greeted by Constable Lachine. "We've been looking for you, Sarah," he says, smiling. "Get in."

"I'm soaking wet and dirty."

"It doesn't matter. We're just happy to find you." He takes her hand and pulls her onto the high seat. She closes the door and hears the lock click. "We'll take care of you now, Sarah." As he speaks, she hears chuckling from the back seat and turns to see her captors.

"No," she screams and tries to open the door, but the SUV is moving quickly, leaving a trail of dust behind.

"I've never heard of a barn in the forest," Lonnie said as they entered the Caroline Dormon Trail at the Scenic Byway. "I've ridden this trail a lot, but never saw a barn. Hope the reverend got it right."

"She doesn't miss much," Dave said, wondering whether Lonnie knew that the reverend was his wife.

"Well, she said she got hurt on the horse trail and I've only ridden the ATV trail. This'll be a new ride for me. Let's see what we can find." He revved up the borrowed Kawasaki Mule and hit the trail.

"Is this an ATV?" Dave asked.

"Sort of, it's a cross between an ATV and a utility four-wheeler. My friend uses it on his dad's farm."

"The ATV ambulance picked Donna up near the end of the trail, and then took her on a service road not open to the public. They met a regular ambulance at the Scenic Byway."

"This must be the service road," Lonnie said as they reached the end of the Dormon Trail. "Let's see where it leads."

"Look," Dave said, pointing to an old barn on the north side of the service road. "It's an old log and board barn, probably early 19th century. I've never seen anything like it in New England. Same function—hay loft on the upper level and animal stalls on the lower, but it's short, maybe fifteen feet high."

"Looks like someone's still using it," Lonnie said. "There's smoke coming out of a chimney."

"Barns don't usually have chimneys," Dave said.

"This one does. Didn't the reverend see smoke?"

"As a matter of fact, she did."

"Doesn't smell like wood smoke, though. Wonder what they're burning?" Lonnie asked.

"Let's find out," Dave said, as they turned the ATV onto the rough roadway toward the barn.

"I think we have a greeter," Dave said, pointing to a young man stepping out of an open doorway.

"Hold it right there," the man shouted. "Whatcha want?"

Continuing to approach the man, Dave said, "I'm Ranger Dave Kraft."

"I said hold it right there. Don't come any closer, Ranger. We don't want people nosing around here."

"We're not 'nosing' around. We're searching for a young woman who disappeared, and we would like to ask some questions about a recent homicide. Can we speak to the owner?"

"He ain't here, and we don't know nothin' about them things. You better be leavin'." He placed his hand in his denim jacket.

"Okay, but we'll be back," Dave said.

I check the perimeter of the cleared area while Lauren walks to the vault toilet, a fancy outhouse without plumbing. Halfway there she stops and looks at what appears to me to be a carcass. I can hear flies buzzing around it from fifteen feet away. Lauren calls, "It's a natural kill, Mark—a fawn taken down by a large cat if I'm reading these prints correctly."

"Bigger than a coyote or bobcat," I say. "I've heard there are pumas in these parts."

"Wouldn't want to be around here at night," Lauren says as she pulls open the bathroom door. "Mark, come in here, quickly."

"What is it?"

"Sarah's been here. One of her toe shoes is here, and some other things—bottles and some trash."

"Don't touch anything, Lauren. I'll call Durand."

"Our radios won't make contact with Durand," Lauren says, "and we're several hours from the SUV. We've got to get back."

"No, we can reach Dave on the radio. He's on an ATV with Lonnie. They can get to Durand. We'll wait here, and then get a ride back with the deputy."

"Stay where you are, Mark," Dave says, "in case Sarah returns."

"She's not going to return, Dave. I believe she's been held here and was moved or escaped, but I'll fill you in when you get here."

"I've got a story for you, too, Mark—about the barn."

"Mark, it's not water in the bottles. One empty bottle may have contained water. The other is half full and contains something that smells like some kind of liquor. There are banana peels and wrappers from trail bars and blood stains on the wall." Lauren is trying to keep her cool, but her eyes give her away.

"I think you should go outside. Let me finish here. We're off the case, remember? This case belongs to Pete, Emil, and the deputy."

"Tell another mother, Mark." Lauren braces herself and goes back to work. After examining the bathroom inch by inch she tries to sort out the footprints outside, but pine needles tell no stories.

"Please, not again." I beg the man behind me not to wrap my head in duct tape again, but he won't listen.

"Damn, she stinks," the other man says.

"She won't be in here long," Lachine says.

"What are you going to do with me now?" I ask.

"Be quiet, Sarah," Lachine answers. "I'm not going to hit you like these animals did, but don't test me."

I'm too tired to cry, but not to listen. I pay attention, even guessing the minutes between every sound, every stop, every turn. It's less than an hour when we turn onto loose gravel and stop. All three of the men get out of the car. The two in the back seat take me by my arms and half drag me into a building, then lock the door behind me and leave. It smells like Ace's garage in New Hampshire. Am I alone? No one has taped my hands or feet. I could remove the tape from my head, but is there someone here with me? I can't hear anything except occasional traffic passing outside, then the door opens and someone enters.

"Where is he?" Lauren asks.

"Lauren, I just radioed Dave. He and Lonnie have to get to Dave's car then drive to a phone to call Durand. Durand is thirty minutes away if he's in Natchitoches. He'll still get here before we could walk to the Excursion."

In less than an hour I hear a motor. Leaving a dust trail, Dave and Lonnie come into view on their four-wheeler. "The deputy said he had to clear everything with Pete before he came onto federal property," Dave reports.

"This is going to be a jurisdictional nightmare," I say.

"Doesn't need to be. The kidnapping occurred in Natchitoches making it a civilian matter. Pete could make it difficult if he wanted, I suppose, but I'm sure he's as anxious to find Sarah as we are. Besides, he has two unsolved murders on his plate. That won't get him a promotion."

"How will Durand get past the chain at the camp entrance?" Lauren asks.

"We dropped the chain," Lonnie says. "It wasn't locked, just looped over a post." No sooner had Lonnie spoken than we hear sirens.

After placing crime scene tape around the bathroom, Deputy Durand reorganizes his search parties and directs them to the Kisatchie. Pete does the same with the equine and ATV teams. All teams are ordered to assemble at Red Bluff at sunrise on the following morning.

"How did we miss this on the first go-around?" Durand asks. "It's obvious that Sarah was here during our search."

"We followed the maps that were given to us," Lonnie says.

"Who drew the maps?" Durand asks.

"Pete," I say. "He knows the area better than anyone."

"Back to my question," Durand says.

"I suppose the ranger considered this camp an unlikely place since it's closed for this season," Lonnie says.

"Seems like that would make it the most likely place." Durand says.

"It's just you and me now, Sarah," Lachine says, wrapping a rope around my body, and pinning my arms to my side. He shoves a chair under me and pushes me onto it, then painfully removes the duct tape from my head. The first thing I see when I open my eyes is the constable's gun. "Get on your feet and go through that door."

I was right. It's a garage, a gas station. They've put me in the small office in front of the garage and I can see the road and a hanging traffic light a small distance away. A large gravel parking area separates the station from the road.

The constable pushes me through a door at the rear of the office into a filthy bathroom smelling of urine. At the top of the outside wall I see a window too small to crawl through. "You're going to stay here until I get back, Sarah. I'll bring you some food to eat. There's water here so clean yourself up. You're making everyone sick." He closes and locks the door behind him. No board. This door has a padlock on the outside.

In a moment he knocks on the door and says, "By the way, Sarah, it won't help to yell. This old station's been closed for years. No one comes here and they won't hear you from the road. I know that because you're not the first visitor we've had." I hear him leave the station. "Who else?" I wonder.

I've got to drink some water, Sarah thinks, turning the dripping faucet handle. I find a small dirty bar of soap dried to the sink, pry it loose and spend my first hour giving myself a bath of sorts. Considering everything, it feels wonderful. I drink from my hands until I'm afraid I'll vomit.

With no apparent means of opening the barred window, I look for some way to break the glass without cutting myself, but I find nothing. Cleaner and no longer thirsty, I sit down on the rim of the toilet seat and cry, releasing days of pent up anger and fear.

"Our Sarah's crying," a male voice says lyrically outside the door. I hadn't heard anyone come in. The voice is the man who drove the car at the ballet studio.

"Too bad," the man with him says, laughing. "It's too bad I don't have the key to this lock, Sarah. We could have some fun. You know what I mean?"

For the next hour or so I hear them walking back and forth through the office, opening and closing the outer door. Then I hear car doors close and the sound of wheels in the parking lot. They're moving something back and forth between the gas station and their car.

We ride on Lonnie's contraption to where our Excursion is parked and head toward Natchitoches, hoping to catch Pete in his office. He isn't there, so we go to the apartment to catch up with the others.

"Where's Dave?" Donna asks.

"He and Lonnie are riding the ATV trails around Red Bluff Camp. They'll be home at sunset. A large group of searchers is returning to the Kisatchie at sunrise tomorrow. Did anything come from your interviews?"

"Nothing, but we handed out a fistful of Sarah's pictures to visitors and volunteers. No one has seen Sarah or anything suspicious. It's really a beautiful forest at this time of year."

"I'm going with the searchers tomorrow, Mark," Ace says. "Donna and Millie can stay here to accept calls."

"Now, just because we're married, Mr. Boss Man, doesn't mean that you'll be directing my traffic. I'll go where I darn well please, and that doesn't include sitting on my growing duff and riding out the storm. Donna has to rest her leg, I don't. If it's all right with her, I'm going to get into the action."

"Be my guest, Millie," Donna says with a smile. "I can hold down the fort."

"Ace, I doubt that these forest cops know the area as well as the locals. Why don't you and I track down this constable in Roberval and get the local lowdown. He'll know more about the troublemakers around here than the feds will."

CHAPTER 17

▼

At eleven Lauren and I are both on mental overload and lay awake without speaking. Lauren breaks the silence. "Where was Pete today?"

"I don't know. I wasn't able to reach him on the phone."

"He took you off the case. It seems like he took himself off the case as well. What's with that guy?"

"At first I thought it was southern languor, but now I wonder."

"What's languor?"

"Indifference."

"Not a good attitude for a man who has two homicides on his plate."

"I agree."

"Would it be helpful if we light a fire under the guy?"

"I'm afraid it would fizzle; besides I wouldn't know how to go about it."

"Mark, be honest with me. Is Sarah still alive?"

"Honey, I wish I knew. You know the drill."

"Yep." Lauren rolls my way and I can feel her breasts on my chest and her breath on my neck. I want nothing more than for everything to be right again— Sarah at home, Ace and Millie on their honeymoon, and Dave and Donna on their vacation, but I know that Sarah's getting close to the valley of the shadow.

"Lauren, I have to ask. Is your faith any help to you now?"

"I haven't wanted to sound like a hypocrite, Mark. I've been away from God for a long time, but yes, I'm ready for any help we can get."

"I guess God'll wait 'til we're desperate, Lauren, but I'm sure he'd rather we place our trust in him. You may have been away from God, but God hasn't been away from you. Would it be all right if I pray out loud?" She raises herself onto one elbow and faces me, but doesn't say anything. I take her silence as approval and pray, "Dear God, we're desperate. Our little girl is being held somewhere and we don't know where or what condition she's in. Give her courage and strength to survive. We want her back alive. Help us to have faith, God. Help us find her. Amen." Lauren lies down and I pray a silent prayer of thanks for her. "Good night, honey."

"Good night, Mark."

The uncompromising alarm clock jolts us back to the real world at five o'clock. We've decided to switch teams for this day. Dave and I will be a team; Lauren and Ace another. Donna will stay at the apartment and Millie will visit Emil. The posse is ready for action by quarter to six, except for Millie. She'll drive the convertible to Lachine's office at eight.

The Kisatchie teams search in an ever-widening circle around Red Bluff Camp, but to no avail. By noon the search is called. Ace and Lauren meet with Deputy Durand.

When Dave and I return to the apartment, Millie is back and she's anxious to talk. "I have something of interest. The constable was in his office when I arrived. He's interesting—unattractive, has a whining voice, but he's very professional in appearance and manners. His office is on the San Antonio Trace across from an abandoned gas station—one of those old stations that got shouldered out by the giants. Anyway, he sat at a desk facing the highway. My back was to the window, but I couldn't hold his gaze. He kept looking out the window over my shoulder. I couldn't imagine why, with a beautiful woman sitting in front of him." Millie can say things like that and not break a grin. I love her. "He had nothing of interest to say about Sarah. In fact, it seemed like he wanted to avoid the topic. I asked him why the search teams hadn't checked Red Bluff Camp. He said that it wasn't his job to designate the search areas. Does anyone but you take responsibility around here? Anyway, I thanked him for his time and left. I was eager to see what it was outside the window that occupied his attention. The only thing I could see was the old gas station and a blue car parked at the entrance. I didn't think much about it until I was driving home. Wasn't Sarah taken in a blue car?"

The constable brings a bag of chips and an apple before it gets dark. "You look better, Sarah, and I'm not going to hurt you, but I have to keep you quiet for awhile."

"Why are you doing this?"

"I told you not to ask questions, remember?"

"I won't, I promise, but …" He raises his hand, and then stops.

"I'm not in a good mood, Sarah. Don't make me do something we'd both regret. I brought a blanket, and I'm also going to give you something to help you sleep. If you fight me on this, I'll pour it down your throat, so cooperate and you'll have a nice, long sleep." He takes a bottle of clear liquid from a paper bag, and removes the cap. "Sit down, Sarah," he says, pointing to the toilet. "Do you want to drink it, or should I pour it down your throat? I understand you're good at chugging booze."

"No, please don't make me drink that stuff. I won't make any noise, I promise." He's already pulling my head back by my hair. "I'll drink some. Don't make me gag."

"More," he says. I drink more. He lifts the bottle while I'm drinking and makes me swallow large gulps. "Now, have a nice night, Sarah."

"My God, Dave, I've been a fool. Would you get everyone in the kitchen? I've got to think." The posse forms while I'm experiencing my epiphany. What a dolt I am. Why couldn't I put two and two together and come up with four? I sit in the kitchen, my head resting on my hands at the table.

"Well, it's been a long day, Ranger. Are you going to make us stand here all night?" I don't respond to Millie which makes everyone uneasy.

"Are you okay, Mark?" Lauren asks.

"It's Emil," I say. "He's the key to finding Sarah."

"Emil?" Ace asks. "How do you know?"

"Deduction, my dear Watson, deduction. Hear me out. Millie saw a blue car parked at an abandoned gas station across from Emil's office." I have their attention. "Sarah was abducted in a blue car."

"That's it? That's your epiphany? There are a lot of blue cars, Mark," Lauren says.

"Not really. How many blue cars have you seen recently? And how many of those are Emil gazing at from his office window? Anyway, it's just the beginning of a whole series of incidents that point to Emil. Let's go into the living room where we can sit down. Hear me out, please, then you'll understand why I think Emil is behind Sarah's disappearance. Millie, keep notes, please."

"Whatever you say, boss." Millie leaves the room and returns with writing material. She wiggles herself onto the couch between Dave and Donna, and takes a magazine from the coffee table. "I'm ready."

"I'm going back in time. My thoughts are still forming, so bear with me. When I came here I was prepared to investigate the death of Beth Beckett, but then I learned of a previous death under similar circumstances—Lovely Hampden. The investigation of her death was cut short, partly at the insistence of Emil Lachine who joined Lovely's parents in demanding that the body be cremated, even before a complete examination could be made—an understandable request from parents, but not from a law enforcement officer. At the inquiry there was insufficient evidence to make a finding of homicide because of the cremation and sloppy police work. Providentially, Lovely's mother requested and got a lock of her hair. I had some of that hair tested and it revealed a high level of alcohol in Lovely's body. When I mentioned to Emil that I was also investigating Lovely's death, he went pale."

"You never told me that," Lauren says.

"It didn't register as important then, but there's more. Shortly after I arrived, students at Sarah's school tried to recruit her into their fringe group by getting her to drink alcohol, but their plan backfired. Sarah drank too much too fast and wound up in an alcoholic coma and nearly died. When I tried to find out who was responsible, Emil intervened with Pete. I was told to back off. Then when I confronted Emil, he told me that Sarah was the problem."

"Blaming Sarah doesn't logically lead to kidnapping her," Dave says.

"Stay with me, Dave, I'm not through. After I got the name of the witness to Sarah's incident, I went to see her. She'd been beaten into silence. Then one of the boys who accosted Sarah was killed with another boy in a staged auto accident. Someone silenced them before I could get to the bottom of the issue. One of the boy's cell phones was stolen, presumably at the accident scene, and was then used to make a threatening call to me. Dave was there when I received the call. Emil had been at the accident scene, and may have been involved in setting up the accident."

"That's a matter for another day, Mark," Donna says. "Right now, Sarah's our concern." Lauren is standing behind the couch. Donna reaches back and takes her hand.

"After the accident some classes were cancelled so students could receive counseling. I took Sarah, but she was more interested in seeing Lonnie. She knew that Lonnie would have inside information about the accident. While she was looking for Lonnie, I located Emil in the parking lot of the school. He was huddling with three young men, not students, who quickly jumped into a pickup truck and sped away as I approached. It seemed odd at the time, but I let it go."

"What's the significance of that?" Ace asks.

"I'm not sure, but I think it's a piece of the puzzle."

"Are you suspecting Lonnie, too?" Lauren asks.

"I don't think so, but I'm not closing that door. Lonnie's been close to Sarah and to our family. He's probably told Emil things about our goings-on, innocently perhaps, but Emil has an inside source on our activities; anyway, when I mentioned the alcohol problem at the school. Emil deferred to another matter."

"Can you connect Emil to our episode at Toledo Bend?" Lauren asks.

"I was getting to that, but since you brought it up, here's what I think. I dismissed the report that Emil's fingerprints were on the gas can because he's a fisherman. It seemed more unlikely that Pete's would be on the can since Pete doesn't fish. Now, I recall informing Emil on the night before that we'd be going out on the lake the following morning. Nothing happened on the first day, probably so that we wouldn't expect any problems if we went out again. As we know, someone drilled holes in the bottom of the boat then placed an empty gas can over the holes. It would have been easy for Emil to do these things while we slept because the boat was on a trailer in front of our apartment."

"Why would he do such a thing?" Millie asks.

"I'm not sure yet. He obviously didn't want me involved in the investigation of Sarah's incident. He didn't want me probing into the auto accident or asking questions about the alcohol problem at the school. He was shocked at my involvement in Lovely Hampden's death, and he was absolutely no help in the investigation of Beth Beckett's death. That brings me to another issue. When I began my investigation of Ms. Beckett's death, the ME's report wasn't available. It was at Emil's house. Why? Why would a constable of a small town want the ME's report of a death on federal property, especially given his obsession over jurisdictional boundaries? Eventually, I got the ME's report, but Emil had it sidetracked for awhile."

"Things are adding up, Mark. Keep going," Dave says.

"Wait a minute, Mark," Millie says. "I didn't mention this, but when I asked Emil why we hadn't searched Red Bluff Camp, he put the blame on Pete, saying he just followed the map he was given."

"That's interesting, because Emil knows Kisatchie better than Pete. He hunts and fishes there on a regular basis, especially near Red Bluff Camp. Emil would know that a closed camp would be a better place to hide someone than one that's open, especially at this busy season. Thanks, Millie."

"What do we do now, Mark?" Lauren asks.

CHAPTER 18

▼

"We have to move fast. Every minute counts if we're to find Sarah in time. I'll call Pete. Lauren, you call Deputy Durand. We'll tell them what we've discussed and what we're going to do. Hopefully, they'll be able to help. Dave and I will find Emil. Donna and Millie, please stay at the apartment. We'll need you to act as a command center, especially if we locate Sarah. Ace, you work with Lauren and Durand. Everyone on board? Be sure to keep your cell phones turned on. Dave, did you bring your service weapon?"

"Never without it, Mark."

"Let's go. I'll call Pete on the way." As federal law enforcement officers, Dave and I are authorized to carry concealed weapons. Since we're out of federal jurisdiction, we leave our service weapons at the apartment and carry our own pistols. Each of us owns a Glock 19 semi-automatic 9mm pistol which we carry in a predator holster on our belt. This holster gives up the weapon quickly and is easily concealed behind a waist length jacket. Lauren surrendered her service revolver when she left New Hampshire and has never owned a private weapon. Dave and I are leaving our service weapons, so I give Lauren the key to the gun cabinet, just in case.

"Come on, Mark, the Saints are cleaning Seattle's clock. What could be important enough to interrupt that?" Pete asks.

"Sorry to disturb your game, Pete, but you'd better hear this. I believe Constable Lachine is somehow involved in Sarah's abduction. Dave and I are looking for him now."

"Lachine? No way. Do you have evidence?"

"Mostly circumstantial at this point, Pete, but when you put it all together, it tells a story."

"Where are you now?"

"On six, headed for Roberval, about four miles from his trailer."

"Keep me informed, Mark. You're out of our jurisdiction, you know."

"Lauren is talking to Deputy Durand as I speak."

The town of Roberval is on the way to Lachine's place. I tell Dave about Lachine's speeding scheme. One way to pull Lachine out of the bushes is to race through the sleepy town and run their only red light, the light between the abandoned gas station and Lachine's office. Luck is not on our side. The light is flashing yellow and the gas station and office are dark as we fly by. We proceed west to Lachine's place.

The day is a blur. I sit with my back against the wall trying to focus my eyes. Every time the constable comes he makes me drink more alcohol, which I vomit as soon as he leaves, like a bulimic. It doesn't keep me sober, but at least I get rid of some of it. I'm so weak that I can't even shout, and when I do my words all run together. The traffic light outside the station flashes on and off at night. At first, it didn't bother me, but tonight, with my head swimming, it's like water torture. Someone's coming.

"Hello, Sarah," I hear the constable's helper saying, his words getting louder as they approach the bathroom. They taunt me through the door, but I know they don't have keys, so I'm not worried. To my surprise, the door opens.

Lonnie answers the door. "Is your father home"? I ask.

"Nope, something wrong? Is Sarah okay?"

"We don't know, Lonnie. We need to talk to the constable."

"The constable ain't here," Lettie says, pushing Lonnie to the side.

"Do you know where he is?" Dave asks.

"Who are you?"

"This is Ranger David Kraft, Mrs. Lachine. Do you know where Constable Lachine is? We need to talk to him."

"We got a new ranger around here?"

"He's on vacation from New England. Please, Mrs. Lachine, tell me where I can find your husband."

"He made one of his rare appearances for dinner tonight, but then the phone rang and he shot out of here like a cannon ball. Never said where he was going. If you catch up to him, tell him we thank him for stopping by." She closes the door.

"Where to now, Mark?" Dave asks.

"Let's visit a gas station."

As I roar into Roberval, I see a blue sedan parked outside the station. There are no lights in the station, office, or car, so I switch off my headlights and pull to the side of the building. I call Durand from my SUV and ask him to send help then Dave and I, armed with flashlights in our left hands and Glock 19's in our right, go in opposite directions around the building.

Constructed of concrete block, the station is typical of those from the mid-1900's. It has two service bays, a front office for serving customers, a room in the back, probably a private office, and a bathroom. The gravel parking lot surrounds the front and sides. There's one window on each side wall approximately eight feet high. We meet in the back which is overgrown with weeds and littered with discarded pallets, buckets, and rusting auto parts.

"No sounds or lights, Mark. I think the place is empty, but the window on my side is open." Dave whispers.

"Let's go inside." I get duct tape from my toolbox, spread it over the window pane above the front door handle, then break and remove the glass. In a minute we're inside. Dave protests mildly until I gave him a "this is my daughter" stare. He relents. We turn on the lights and split up again. I go into the service bays; Dave goes to the rear of the front office. We hit pay dirt just as two patrol cars with sirens blaring come through the flashing light and skid to a stop. Durand steps out of one and another deputy steps out of the other. Both adjust their personal equipment and move toward the broken front door.

"Looks like a break-in," Durand says as I meet him at the door.

"I broke the window to get in," I say. "Dave Kraft and I are looking for Sarah."

"She's been here," Dave says, coming from the rear. "Come with me." He leads us through an opening to a short hallway with a door on each side. One leads to a small cluttered office, the other to a bathroom. Dave steps aside and Durand steps in.

"Don't come in here, please, just look. There's evidence that someone was living here. It may have been Sarah." He directs the other deputy to tape the entrance to the bathroom. "Whoever was here left in a hurry. There's half a warm hot dog on the sink."

Durand steps out and I step in before the tape goes up. A cotton blanket is rolled up in the corner of the bathroom and a paper sack containing several items of clothing is behind the door. The stench of vomit and something vaguely familiar permeates the room. In the sack are two worn pairs of women's underpants and an unopened package containing four new pairs. On the sink is a sample tube of toothpaste, a toothbrush, a used bar of soap, and a dirty hand towel. "Whoever left was a woman and she went in a hurry, leaving her toiletries."

"She was here against her will," Dave says. "Look at the wall." Written on the back of the door in toothpaste are the words "help me sa."

"She didn't finish her message," Durand says.

"Yes, she did," I say. "Her name is Sarah Adams."

"There's something else I want you to see in the service bays," I say to Deputy Durand. He follows me to the other side of the gas station. I turn on the overhead lights. Stacked on pallets are unmarked cardboard boxes, each containing four gallon bottles of clear liquid. "Want to guess what's in these bottles?" I ask. "Remember what we were offered at the Cellar Saloon, Dave?"

"Panther's Breath," Dave says.

"Right, it's what I smelled in the bathroom. Sarah's been drinking and vomiting Panther's Breath. They've kept her drunk."

"Isn't this the girl with the drinking issue?" Durand asks.

"Let's get this straight, Deputy, my daughter has no drinking problem that isn't forced on her."

"Sorry. Looks like it's been forced on her again."

"You can bet this is the distribution center for the alcohol that's been causing problems in your parish, deputy, and the blue car in front is probably the transport vehicle. This solves one of your problems, but right now I'm only interested in my problem—finding Sarah."

"Sounds like you've got your priorities in order, Mark. You stay here," Durand says to his deputy. "Arrange to have this moonshine and car moved to impound and get the investigative team out here. I've got a hostage to find."

My cell phone chirps as Dave and I are getting into the Excursion. "Lettie Lachine called," Lauren says. "She wants you to talk to Lonnie. Can you get out to her place? It sounds important."

"We're close to Sarah, honey. She was at the abandoned gas station in Roberval, but she's been moved again. We just left Durand at the station. Dave and I'll go to Lachine's, but I hope it's important." It takes less than fifteen minutes to get back to Lachine's. Lonnie steps outside to meet us.

"What's up, Lonnie? Your mother called and said you wanted to talk to us." He looks troubled.

"I don't know if it's important, but when you were here earlier you sounded like you were onto something. I was doing homework in the kitchen when my dad got the call." Lonnie pauses.

"What call?"

"The call just before he left. He got real pale and threw the phone down on the table, then left in a hurry."

"Is that it, Lonnie? Is that what you wanted to talk about?"

"There's more. He was talking real soft, but before he threw the phone down I heard him say something about a barn, and then he ran out."

"What barn?" Dave asks.

"That's just it. I don't know anything about any barn. We don't have one or have any friends with barns, then I remembered the barn in the forest—the one that we went to, Ranger Kraft. They weren't very friendly there, were they?" Dave looks at me.

"Does your mother know what that was about?"

"I didn't say anything to my mother. I wanted to tell you, just in case it helps find Sarah."

"You did the right thing, Lonnie. Let's keep this to ourselves for now, okay? And thanks." Dave and I hurry to the SUV.

"Can you direct us to the barn in the dark?" I ask Dave.

"The service road near the barn exits on the Scenic Byway. I don't remember any markers at that intersection, but it's west of the Caroline Dormon trailhead. If we get to the trailhead we've gone too far."

"Call Pete on your cell phone while we've got service. Tell him where we're headed. Have him meet us there with help, if possible. Put the phone on speaker." Dave dials the Toussant house. Pete answers.

"We're on Sarah's trail, Pete. She was at the old gas station in Roberval, but was moved just before we got there. We think Lachine may be at the old barn near the Dormon trail in the Kisatchie. We'll notify Deputy Durand, and we'll need help from you and whoever you can muster."

"We also found a stash of Panther's Breath at the gas station, Pete. Sheriff Hardman was right about the moonshine," I shout toward the phone.

"When you get there, Rangers, do nothing until I arrive, do you understand?" Pete says. I make no promises.

"We'll see you there," I answer. Dave pushes the off button then calls the apartment. Lauren answers.

"Lauren, listen carefully," I say, "call Deputy Durand. You'll need to use your cell phone. He's on the move. Tell him we're headed to an old barn near the Dormon trail—the one Donna saw after her accident. Lonnie heard Emil refer to a barn on the phone before we arrived at his place. That's what he wanted to tell us. We think Emil may have Sarah there. I've notified Pete, but he's been operating in low gear. Durand may have a jurisdictional problem, but we need all the help we can get."

"I'm coming, too, Mark."

"No, Lauren, please. We're dealing with some pretty ugly people and we're in strange territory."

"Mark, 'no' is not in my vocabulary right now. I have as many years in law enforcement as you and I've dealt with some ugly characters in my career. I'll leave Donna and Millie here. I'm sure my father will want to be with me. We'll bring your service pistols, just in case. Donna can give me directions. I'll call Durand on the way." The phone goes dead. She doesn't wait for an argument. I can't tell her she can't search for her daughter.

CHAPTER 19

▼

"Daddy, we're going on a hunt. Can you handle a pistol?"

"Honey, you're looking at the man who's still on record in New Hampshire for killing the biggest buck with a black powder gun. If I can handle black powder, I can handle a pistol. Bring it on. Where are we going?"

"To an old barn in the Kisatchie."

"Is it the barn I saw?" Donna asked.

"That's the one," Lauren said as she opened Mark's gun cabinet. "Mark must have his belt holster, Dad, but Dave's and Mark's service holsters are here. Strap this on and I'll load the magazines while we're on the road. We'll need to take the convertible."

"Where's Millie?" Ace asked as he and Lauren headed for the kitchen door and the driveway.

"Don't know," Donna answered, "possibly in the bathroom."

"Fill her in, please," Ace called over his shoulder. "Tell her I'll be back, hopefully with our little girl."

"Will do."

"I'll drive," Ace said. "You navigate. You've been to the Dormon trail, I haven't, okay?" They jumped into the convertible and spun out of the driveway. Just as they turned onto Highway Six, Lauren heard a shuffling sound in the rear seat.

My head is spinning and I hurt everywhere. The constable and his two friends have thrown me into the police car. In the back seat, with a man on each side, I can't see where we're going nor do I care. If they're going to kill me, I wish they would do it now. I can't take another night. The alcohol they pour into my mouth is a welcome relief.

"She's asleep or something," one of the men said to Lachine.

"How much did you give her?"

"Not that much."

"She had a lot in her already. I don't want her dead, understand?"

"Why not? She can identify all of us now."

"She's still our ticket out of this mess."

"You're kidding yourself. We'd be better off dumping her in the bayou like the others and getting the hell out of Louisiana."

"Keep your mouth shut. She may be able to hear this."

"I'm getting tired of your orders. We do all your dirty work and all we get is your grief. What's in this for us?"

Lachine pulled the car to the shoulder of the Byway. "Get out," he said to the man, pointing a pistol at his head.

"No, I didn't mean what I said. I'm sorry."

"You're sorry, all right," Lachine said, firing one shot into the back of the man's head and kicking his collapsing body into the ditch alongside the Byway. He returned to the car. "You got anything you want to say?" Lachine asked the other man. With a frozen look on his face and his mouth agape, he shook his head slowly.

"I know that old barn," Pete said to Deputy Durand. "There's nothing out there. No reason to get excited. I'm on the way to the Kisatchie now. I'll let you know if we need any help. This is my jurisdiction, Deputy. I'm sure I can handle it with three rangers."

"You haven't handled the two homicides in the Kisatchie, Toussant," Durand said.

"I don't need to be reminded, Durand. As you know, that investigation is still open and we'll get the job done."

"I'm going to stand by tonight just the same, in case you need help."

"Suit yourself."

The gunshot startles me. I struggle to clear my head. "What happened?"

"Go back to sleep," the man next to me says.

"Where's the other guy?" I ask, not certain that I really want to know.

"Shut up."

"She's not out yet," the constable says, "give her some more." The man grabs my hair and pulls my head back, forcing me to take more of the alcohol.

"No," I say, "I'm getting sick."

"Puke on me and you'll clean it up. Just go to sleep."

"Where are you, Mark?" Lauren asks.

"I'm just turning into the forest. Where are you?"

"We left the apartment a minute ago, but we have an issue."

"What's the issue?"

"After we got on the road, Millie popped up in the back seat. She was hiding under a blanket."

"I was not hiding. I was resting," Millie shouts into the phone.

"We don't have time to take her back, Mark."

"Have Ace keep an eye on her. I don't want her to get hurt."

"He heard that. I've got the speaker on."

"Millie, no Agatha Christie stuff. I mean it. I've got all I can handle without worrying about you."

"Okay, Ranger, but remember who saved your sorry self in New Hampshire."

"I remember—got to go." I don't know whether she hears that or not. My cell phone goes out of service as we enter the forest.

"The service road intersects the byway west of the Dormon trailhead. It should be up here in about a mile or two, on the right. It's unpaved and narrow in spots, Mark. Are you sure we can do it in this mammoth?"

"The Excursion's large, Dave, but I've got four-wheel drive if we need it and a diesel V-8. If we can squeeze through the narrows, we'll be okay. I'd rather try it than have to walk."

"Ace won't make it in his convertible."

"I forgot about that. We'll wait at the intersection and take them with us." As we approach the service road I pull to the side and wait. "They can't be more than twenty minutes behind us."

"There has to be auto or truck access to the barn, Dave. I just don't know where it is. You were there. Did you and Lonnie see cars?"

"No cars. There was a rough dirt drive leading from the service road to the barn. The barn was ancient, been there since horse and wagon times."

"Can't believe there's not another way to get to it." Headlights approach from the rear. I expect either Pete or Ace. It's Ace. He pulls onto the shoulder behind me and steps out of the convertible.

"What gives?" he asks.

"Dave and I think it would be better to leave the convertible here and take the Excursion. More power and more traction."

"It's awfully big, Mark."

"Let's give it a try. Climb in." Ace and Lauren climb up to the back seat and leave Millie standing alongside.

"Well?" Millie asks, looking at Ace. Chagrined, he gets out and gives Millie a boost.

"Life was easier when I was single," Ace mumbles.

"I heard that," Millie says. I turn onto the service road.

"Frankly, I don't give a hoot about jurisdiction, Sheriff," Durand says to his boss. "Toussant is dragging his feet on finding the girl and we've already got two unsolved homicides in the forest."

"It's the forest, Deputy. We have to be invited. If Toussant thinks he can handle the search, that's his call."

"I know you and Toussant are friends, but he has too few rangers and they're not trained for this kind of work."

"I thought Ranger Garrison and his wife were former cops."

"They are, but Toussant has their hands tied, playing jurisdictional games."

"He's probably on thin ice with his supervisors because his homicide investigations are dragging."

"I say we get out there and do what we can to help and let the personalities and politics sort themselves out."

"All right, but I'm going to cover your back. I'll get in touch with Toussant's supervisor in the morning. Now, tell me what you have in mind."

I wake up when they drag me from the police car, but everything in my head is swimming. All I know is that my feet are bouncing along the ground and my shoes have fallen off. They drop me onto the ground and leave me there. When I try to stand up I fall on my side. In a few minutes they come back and drag me through a doorway. The smell is awful.

"Lay her down in the office," the constable says. Someone covers me with a blanket then leaves me in the dark room.

"Did you bring your pistols?" I ask.

"Yes, and they're loaded," Lauren replies.

"I don't have one," Millie says.

"And that's how it's going to stay," I reply.

"Annie Oakley saved your life once, Ranger."

"I'll never forget it, either, Millie. I owe my life to you, but Annie is in New Hampshire and I've run out of weapons."

The SUV suffers a few scratches driving through the narrow spots, but it gets us to within a hundred yards of the barn. It's hard to keep a diesel engine quiet, so when we're in sight of the barn, I turn it off. "We'll go the rest of the way on foot. Millie, do you think you can drive this thing?"

"You're asking an old farmwoman whether she can drive on a dirt road? That's like asking a ranger whether he can hike in the woods. Just give me the keys and tell me the plan."

"Once we leave I want you to get behind the wheel and watch the barn. If you see me flash my light three times, you'll know that we've got Sarah and are in control. Then you get this thing as close to the barn as you can, okay? In the meantime, keep the doors locked and the motor and lights off. The rest of you, come with me." I lead Dave, Lauren, and Ace to within one hundred feet of the entrance to the barn. Lights are shining through the loft and door openings and there's a strong smell in the air.

"What's the smell, Mark?" Dave asks.

"You boys are young, aren't you?" Ace says. "That's the smell of a still. Someone's making moonshine in that barn."

"In the middle of the night?" I ask.

"Depends on where they are in the process. If they're heating the mash, they have to stay with it until it's done. It's easy to ruin a batch. By the smell, I'd say they're in production."

"You seem to know a lot about it, Ace," Dave says.

"I take the fifth," Ace says.

"He did that too often," Lauren whispers. "Don't ask Dad about his history with booze."

"Sorry," Dave says.

"Lauren, you and Dave move as close as you can to the front door, but stay hidden. Ace, come with me. We'll circle the building. Everyone stay as quiet as possible."

Ace and I make our way around the old barn. The moon is near full and the sky is clear, so it isn't necessary to use our flashlights. The Kisatchie forest has little scrub or ground level vegetation, so we move among the tall pine trees until we've returned to Lauren and Dave.

"What did you see?" Dave whispers.

"There's a double door at the far end of the building, and, as you can see, a double and single door at this end. Three fairly new Kawasaki Mules are parked in the back."

"No one was in sight," Ace says. "Apparently, we weren't heard." As if to put a lie to Ace's observation, the Excursion's diesel engine comes alive and we watch in surprise as the SUV roars out of sight.

"Stay down," I say. Seconds later, the small door in front of the building opens and Emil Lachine steps outside holding a hand gun at eye level. He shakes his left fist in anger and steps backward into the barn. In less than a minute, the front and rear of the barn are illuminated by fixtures mounted under the eaves at the peak of the roof.

"Millie was in the Excursion," Ace says.

"Let's all retreat to the road to see whether she got out," I say. There's no sign of Millie.

"At the speed the driver left, he won't make it far on the service road. Do any of you know how to drive a Mule?" No one responds.

"Ace, you know where they are. Take Dave and see if they left a key in one of the Mules. If so, go after the SUV. Lauren, cover them at the rear of the building. I'm going in through the front."

"We should wait for Pete," Lauren says.

"Sarah is in there, Lauren. Do you really want to wait?"

The Mule coasts quietly over pine needles until it's on the service road. The four-stroke engine starts quickly. At a governed speed of 25 mph, Ace goes searching for Millie and the Excursion. Dave rejoins me in the front of the barn. We wait ten minutes for some action from Lachine, but there is none. Just as we're about to make our way to the front door, a gun fires behind us and the front light explodes. In seconds another shot darkens the rear light. As we turn to see who's firing, Millie joins us, followed by Ace. The barn door swings open and Lachine opens fire from the doorway, shooting into the darkness.

"What in the world is going on?" Dave asks.

"There's a young man in the back seat of your tank, Mark. He didn't expect to find anyone. He got the heavy end of my cane and is now hog-tied in your backseat. I can also tell you that your expensive car isn't in very good shape. My brave husband rescued me."

"Where did you get the gun, Millie?" I ask.

"Ace laid it on the front seat of his go-cart and I took it. Are we going to have this chat all night?"

"Millie, go with Ace to the back of the barn and check on Lauren. Dave and I are going inside."

I'm awakened by gunfire outside the barn and try to sit up, but everything is spinning. I choke on my vomit then roll onto my stomach. My face is lying in blood and my skin feels cold. As the door opens my whole body starts shaking, then everything goes black.

"Okay, Sarah, this is how it's going to be. You and I are going for a ride in the woods, just like Little Red Riding Hood, except we're not going to Grandma's house. We're going to take a cool dip in Bayou Pierre. Sarah, wake up, WAKE UP."

The small barn door is locked from the inside. I try the double door. It, too, is locked. "Ace, get the Mule," I say. "See if you can break down the double door. Dave and I'll cover you." Ace retrieves the Mule and rams the double door, but it doesn't budge. He rams it a second time and the doors part enough for us to walk through. Ace ducks out of sight as Dave and I follow our pistols into the old building.

Ace is right. There is a still operating in the barn, but not of the early style— car radiators and 55-gallon drums. This still looks like a modern mini-brewery with stainless steel vessels and pipes. These bootleggers are big time operators. An automated bottling machine is operating, but is spilling its product on the concrete floor. No one has put empty bottles on the line. Apparently, the machine operator is now hog-tied in my SUV. It appears that Emil and Sarah are the only people in the barn.

We hear Lauren's voice from the woods behind the building. "Hold it right there," she shouts as Lachine exits the double door carrying Sarah. He quickly retreats inside and latches the door behind him. We have him trapped inside, but he has Sarah.

Dave and I move toward the rear of the barn, using the old stalls for cover, keeping our eyes toward the rear door. Emil comes into view above us, climbing the steps of a rolling ladder next to a large vessel. Sarah is hanging motionless in his arms. "I have you in my sights, Lachine. Stop where you are. Put Sarah down and come down the steps. I won't shoot unless I have to."

"You can shoot if you like, Ranger. I'm standing over a vessel of mash that's 170 degrees. If you shoot me now Sarah goes headfirst into happyland. I'd suggest that you and whoever is with you come out here where I can see you. Toss your weapons into a stall then lay face down. I'm going to count to ten. If I don't see you before I get to ten, Sarah dies."

Dave and Ace look at me. "Toss your weapons. Move into the open where he can see us. I think he's desperate enough to drop Sarah."

"Don't be stupid, Lachine. We're moving toward you. We've tossed our weapons. Don't make this worse for yourself. Bootlegging isn't a capital crime, but murder is."

"Thanks for the lecture. Now, tell whoever is outside to come through the double doors without their guns and stand in the doorway where I can see them. Do it now. This girl is getting heavy."

I walk to the double door with my hands above my head, keeping myself where Lachine can see me. "I'm going to open the door, Lauren. Come to the opening without your weapon. Lachine is threatening Sarah. Do as I say." I emphasize Lauren's name, hoping that Millie won't respond. Lauren comes to the door with her hands in the air.

"Mrs. Garrison, get into that Mule next to you and start the engine. Leave it running and then stand by your husband and the others." Lauren does as she's told. "In the stall behind you is some rigging. Take a coiled rope and tie the men to the post next to them. Don't play games with me, Mrs. Garrison, and don't waste time. I can't hold Sarah much longer and I'm sure as hell going to drop her if you take too long." Lauren ties Ace, Dave, and me loosely to the post, then looks up at Lachine.

"They aren't going anywhere. Now, put Sarah down and leave. I won't try to stop you."

"It isn't that simple, Ma'am." Lachine says, fumbling for the pistol in his belt holster while hoisting Sarah over his shoulder. Dave and Ace gasp as Sarah's head flops over Lachine's shoulder above the vat. "You're going with me. I'm going to come down the ladder. You're going to walk ahead of me and get into the drivers seat of the Mule, then we're going to drive away from here. When I'm ready, I'll let you and Sarah go. No one needs to get hurt if you do what you're told. Now, start moving toward the Mule." Lauren obeys and Lachine starts down the stairs.

CHAPTER 20

▼

As Lachine reaches the bottom step, a single shot is fired into his forehead. Sarah falls to the ground with a thud and Lachine tips backwards, eyes and mouth wide open. Expecting Millie to walk through the double door, we're all surprised to see Pete Toussant, pistol in hand, with Millie at his side. "Mrs. Garrison," he says. "Do you own that convertible on the Scenic Byway?"

"It's a rental—my father has the keys. Why?"

"I want you and your father to put Sarah in the Mule and drive her to the Mustang, and then rush her to the hospital in Natchitoches. Leave now. If you think she's too sick, call for help when you get a cell signal and have an ambulance meet you. Do you understand?" Lauren nods and runs toward Sarah. Toussant unties the men and helps carry Sarah to the Mule, then watches as Ace and Lauren pull away.

My Excursion is not as badly damaged as I expect. The young man hog-tied in the back has driven it into a pine tree, but the Excursion is tough and the tree gets the worst of the deal. I leave Pete in the barn with Lachine's body. Dave and I help Millie into the SUV and head for the Scenic Byway.

"Did anyone tell Ranger Toussant about this bundle in the back?" Millie asks. I feel like a fool. All of us had forgotten about the man squirming in the rear of the SUV.

"It'll have to wait until we get to Natchitoches. I'll turn him over to Deputy Durand on the way to the hospital," I say. Dave climbs to the cargo area of the SUV to make certain that the suspect is restrained, and removes a driving glove from the man's mouth.

"Cut me loose," the man says. "My hands are numb."

"You'll be cut loose when we get to Natchitoches," Dave says. "What were you doing out here?"

"I'm not saying anything."

"Dave, don't ask anything until you Mirandize him. Let's not jeopardize his pearls of wisdom." Dave delivers the Miranda speech.

"What kind of cop are you?" the man asks Dave.

"Ranger Garrison and I are Forest Service Rangers. We enforce the law in these parts, young man. We'll put you in the custody of civilian authorities until we can sort out the jurisdictional issues. Believe me, we have the right to arrest you and turn you over to either civilian or federal authorities for prosecution. You don't have to say anything, as I said, but it would help your case if you level with us now, especially if anyone else is at risk. You're already involved in a tax evasion case and possibly a whole string of other charges, including kidnapping and possibly murder."

"Hold it. I didn't kidnap or kill anyone. I just did what I was ordered to do."

"And what is that?"

"I'm not saying anything else."

"Who ordered you to make and distribute alcohol without paying taxes?"

"The constable, ask him and he'll tell you that we were just obeying orders."

"That might be difficult. He's dead." The young man goes pale.

"Damn," he says. His head drops and he mumbles something that no one can understand.

"What did you say?" I ask as I reach the Scenic Byway and turn onto the paved road.

"Stop the car," the man repeats.

"I'm not stopping for anything," I say. "My daughter is in bad shape. We're going to drop you off at the parish police station, then go straight to the hospital."

"No, the constable shot my friend just up the road. He's lying in a ditch. You'll see. I was scared to death of the constable. He's crazy."

"Do you know exactly where the man is?"

"Not for sure, but it's less than a mile from here on my side of the road. He pushed the guy into the ditch, but you can probably see him from the road." I slow down.

"Millie and Dave, use your flashlights and look for him."

The young man sees his friend first. "That's him," he shouts. I stop, get out, and walk cross the road. I wished I hadn't. His face and neck are shredded by what appear to be teeth and claw marks. Since he's dead, I remove the contents of his pockets and return to the car.

"We'll report him to Pete and Durand when we get cell service. The ME is going to have a field day." I hand the man's personal stuff to Dave.

"What's your name?" Millie asks the man in the back.

"Mitch," he answers.

As I turn onto state road 119, I see Ace's convertible and an ambulance stopped at the side of the road, near Bayou Pierre where Lovely Hampden's and Beth Beckett's bodies were found. They're putting Sarah into the ambulance. I stop behind the convertible as the ambulance pulls away. Lauren goes with Sarah. "We wouldn't have gotten her to the hospital in time, Mark," Ace says, eyes welling. "She wasn't breathing until Lauren did chest compressions and the EMT's arrived." I put my hands on Ace's shoulders and he lets me hold him in a hug while he cries quietly.

"I have to drop off the man Millie hog-tied at Deputy Durand's office, Ace. Then we'll meet you at the hospital."

"How's Millie doing?"

"You should ask her, Ace. She's coming up behind you." Millie takes Ace's hand and leads him to the convertible."

Dave calls Deputy Durand as I hit seventy miles per hour on I-49. I never regain sight of the ambulance on the interstate.

"We left Ranger Toussant at the barn near the Dormon Trail," Dave says. "Constable Lachine's dead and there's another dead man on the Scenic Byway between the Dormon trailhead and the intersection with LA 119. He's not a pretty sight—been dinner for big cats, I believe. The constable and the two young men were involved in a distilling operation in the old barn on the service road near the Dormon trail. They had Sarah. It seems as though Lachine killed the man at the roadside. We saw Ranger Toussant shoot Lachine. Please meet us at your office. We've got a third man restrained in our vehicle and I've got the contents of the dead man's pockets. We need to transfer the suspect into your custody and turn over the personal effects of the dead man. You and Toussant will have to sort out the jurisdictional issues. After we leave you we'll be headed to the hospital. Sarah's on her way there in an ambulance, barely clinging to life."

"I'll be here, Kraft. Sounds like you boys had a big night at the barn. After Sarah gets settled down, I'll need all of you to come to the sheriff's office to make statements. I'll arrange with the ME to get out to the forest to get the bodies, and

I'll drive out to the barn to see whether Toussant wants our help. As for the boot-legging and kidnapping, that'll be a joint investigation. I'll wait here until you arrive."

Deputy Durand is with the sheriff when we arrive at the station. The first order of business for us is Sarah, so we quickly exchange greetings, transfer Mitch and the personal effects of his dead partner to Durand, and start to leave for the hospital. Before leaving the sheriff informs us that he has notified the ATF office in New Orleans. They'll assume responsibility for the bootlegging investigation and disposition of the still and inventory. He expects the FBI and IRS to be involved with the ATF, and plans to meet with Ranger Toussant and the Louisiana State Police to form a joint investigative task force to look into the deaths, including the two girls at Bayou Pierre and Constable Lachine and his associate, and the kidnapping of Sarah Adams. It'll take a few days to get the task force up to speed. In the meantime, the sheriff says, "Ranger Garrison, you take as much time as you need for your family. We'll get your statement when things have settled down with Sarah. Ranger Kraft, we'd like to have your statement tomorrow."

The hospital is less than five minutes from the sheriff's office. As we pull into the emergency parking area we can see Ace's convertible and an ambulance with lights flashing standing at the emergency room receiving dock. We rush to the walk-through door leading into a triage area, but Sarah is nowhere in sight. A nurse greets us and directs us to the second floor nurse's station at the Intensive Care Unit. Stepping off the elevator we enter a hallway. Facing the elevator are double doors and a sign directing visitors to a wall phone. I identify myself and am told that we should wait in the ICU lounge. Someone will come out and speak with us. Ace, Millie, and Lauren are nowhere in sight.

Dave pours himself coffee from a pot in the lounge and brings me a cup. It's the first time either of us has taken a breath for what seem like days. The soft couch and coffee are welcome, but before we can sip, the phone rings. Since we're the only people in the lounge I answer. "Mark," Lauren says, "please come to the coffee shop on the first floor. Millie, Daddy, and I are here. We're getting a sandwich. They wouldn't let us go with Sarah." She sounds exhausted. We take our coffee, walk down one flight of stairs and follow the signs to the coffee shop. Except for a few hospital people, we're the only ones in the coffee shop.

"Do the ICU nurses know where we are?" I ask.

"Yes, and they have my cell phone number as well," Ace answers.

"What's Sarah's condition?"

"Not as bad as it was on the way here," Lauren says. "She stopped breathing in the car so Millie called 911. I did rescue breathing until the EMT's arrived. They put a breathing device on her face and she breathed on her own." Lauren was getting more hyper as she spoke. I put my hand on her wrist and my finger across my lips.

"Slow down, honey. Take a breath. I'm worried about you. You're too stressed out." She collapses into sobs. I excuse us and take her up to the ICU lounge, asking everyone to stay where they were.

"Now, let's take it slowly," I say to Lauren as we settle into a couch in the lounge. Before she can reply, a nurse comes into the lounge with a glass of water and a pill.

"Someone called the nurse's station and said that you were upset, Mrs. Garrison. I have a very mild sedative that will help you relax, if you wish. It won't knock you out just slow you down a bit. Would you like to try it?" Lauren surprises me by reaching for the pill. "I'd suggest that you stay here for awhile to give it a chance to work. I'll be out again to see how you're doing. Mr. Garrison, please let me know if Mrs. Garrison needs more attention."

"I feel like a fool, Mark," Lauren says.

"Lauren, you're a hero. You probably saved Sarah's life. Now it's time for us to be patient. We have to trust God and the medical folks to take care of Sarah. They'll keep us informed and let us know when we can see her. I'm going to go to the nurse's station and see if they can tell us anything, but first I'd like to call Millie to come up here, okay?" Lauren nods. I meet Millie at the elevator. "Lauren's had a sedative and is in the lounge. Please stay with her. I'm going to see if I can get any information about Sarah. I'll be back in a minute."

"I'm sorry, Mr. Garrison," the clerk says. "The doctors are very busy with Sarah right now, but as soon as someone's available we'll come out and talk to you."

"Is she ..." I can't finish the question.

"Going to make it?" the clerk says. I nod. "She's been through a lot, Mr. Garrison, but at the moment she seems to be holding her own. That's about as much as I can tell you." She comes around the desk and walks me back to the lounge. Ace and Dave are with Millie and Lauren.

"I called Donna, Mark." Dave says. "She says that the TV people are already on top of the story and may be showing up at the hospital, so I talked to security and asked that we not be bothered."

"Thanks, Dave." It's going to be a long night.

CHAPTER 21

▼

Lauren is stretched out with her head in my lap when a familiar looking man in green scrubs enters the lounge. "Hello, Ranger Garrison. Do you remember me?" After a pause, he says, "I'm Dr. Ward. I was on the team that treated Sarah when she was here before."

"Of course," I say. "I'm sorry. Much of that night is a blur."

"I'm sure it is. Would you and Mrs. Garrison join me in the family lounge?" We follow Dr. Ward into a small counseling room. He motions for us to be seated then sits across from Lauren. He looks very serious.

"You look worried, Dr. Ward," Lauren says.

"It's very late and I've been up for too many hours. Besides that, I have reason to be a bit worried." Lauren takes my hand. "Sarah's first episode of alcohol poisoning resulted from a single intake of a large volume of alcohol, followed by a quick intervention in the emergency room. We were able to minimize the effect of the alcohol by intercepting some of it before it was absorbed into her blood stream. As you know, the outcome was very good. As far as I know, she's had no lasting effect, yes?"

"Yes," I say, waiting for the bomb to drop.

"This time, however, she has a lot more alcohol in her system. I've been told a little about what happened to her, but I need to know more. What was she drinking and for how long."

"We don't know much either, doctor," I say. "What we do know is that she was moved at least twice after her kidnapping and that containers of moonshine liquor called Panther's Breath were found at the places she was held. It seems as

- 134 -

though her captors were force-feeding the alcohol. We have no way of knowing how much."

"When can we see her, doctor?" Lauren asks.

"It'll be awhile, Mrs. Garrison. I know you're anxious and I wish I could tell you more."

"What can you tell us?"

"Unlike last time we can't stop the ingestion of the alcohol. It's been in her system long enough to be fully processed. We're more concerned about her life systems, especially breathing, heart rate, and brain function. She's breathing now, but the rate is very slow. Her heart is also laboring, and her brain reactions are somewhat erratic, but that's not unusual at this stage and can change. I suggest that you go home and get some rest. I think she's going to make it through the immediate crisis, but we still have to hydrate her, nourish her, clean her wounds, and place her on antibiotics. As before, she'll be an unhappy camper for awhile."

Dr. Ward walks us to the lounge and promises to call if Sarah's condition worsens during the night. Dave has already gone to the apartment. Ace and Millie walk with us to the SUV while we share the news from Dr. Ward then follow us home in the Mustang. Everyone collapses into bed, but sleep comes slowly for Lauren and me.

We've been in bed for just over an hour when the phone rings. Lauren grabs it and hands it to me. "It's Deputy Durand. Does he ever sleep?"

His first words are not encouraging. "We've got a problem," he says. "You need to come to the station." I dress and leave after getting Lauren to promise to call me when she gets a report from the hospital.

"Mitch hasn't stopped talking since you brought him in. You need to know what he's saying."

"Not as much as I need to get some sleep," I reply. "What's he saying?"

"He's waived his right to an attorney and is dictating a confession as we speak, but here's the gist of it: He admits to being present at the killing of Lovely Hampden and Beth Beckett, and to participating in the kidnapping of Sarah, but he claims that he and his cohort were coerced by Constable Lachine, and there's more. He claims that Lachine was not in charge, that Lachine was also following orders. We also have a lot of information on the bootlegging racket they were running. There's a whole network of teenagers involved in this thing. ATF will have their hands full sorting that out. Right now I'm concerned with getting to the top of the pyramid."

"Any clues?" I ask.

"None, and Mitch is clueless, as well. He knows that Emil hesitated whenever a decision was needed, and often disappeared for periods of time. When he returned he had new orders. Someone else was pulling the strings, but there was no one else involved at the barn. Emil and his two associates ran the still."

"I remember Sheriff Hardman telling me that there's a problem in Natchitoches Parish. He didn't say anything about a problem in Caddo Parish. My bet is the bootlegging didn't get very far from here."

"That's helpful. We've had plenty of alcohol related incidents in our parish over the past year and I think we're seeing the cause. I'm going to need your eyes and ears, Mark, as we dig deeper into this thing. I think we've milked Mitch for all he's worth."

In the morning, I'm up early. I leave a note in the kitchen for Lauren. "I've gone to Lachine's trailer to talk to his wife. There's a new twist in the investigation. I won't be more than thirty minutes from the hospital and I'll be in cell phone range."

A car with the call letters of a local television station is in Lachine's driveway as I turn off of Highway 6. And so it begins, I think. Lachine's dog doesn't raise his head as I step up to the front door. Lonnie answers and lets me in. His eyes are red and he looks as though he hasn't slept. "I'm sorry about your dad, Lonnie."

"Me, too. How's Sarah?"

"We don't know, Lonnie. She's in ICU and they're not letting us see her—perhaps today."

"Could I come when she's better?" He looks genuinely concerned.

"Of course, Lonnie," I say, putting my hand on his shoulder. Surprisingly, he moves toward me and gives me a hug. I do a quick mental inventory and decide two things: first, Lonnie is not part of what has happened to Sarah; and second, Emil led a double life. Go figure. "Think I could talk to your mom?"

"Sure." At that moment, Lettie Lachine and a young man in a sweater and jeans walk from behind a kitchen wall. Carrying a small briefcase in his left hand, he extends his right to Lettie, nods toward me and leaves.

"What do you want, Ranger?" Lettie asks, throwing down the gauntlet.

"I'm sorry for that boy Lonnie," Millie said, as she poured coffee for Ace. "He seems like such a nice young man, and I think Sarah has an interest in him. I watched them at the wedding."

"I think you're right," Lauren added.

"It's hard to imagine that Constable Lachine was able to run a bootlegging operation without his family being involved," Donna said.

"I think that's exactly what he did," Dave said. "Some people can compartmentalize their lives."

"Mark's with the family now," Lauren said. "We'll know more when he gets back."

"He hasn't had a decent night's sleep in several days," Millie said.

"Who has?" Lauren asked. "I'm going to the hospital cafeteria for breakfast, and then I'm going to camp outside of Sarah's door until somebody tells me something. This waiting is killing me."

"Want company?" Ace asked.

"Thanks, Daddy."

"Maybe we could all go," Donna said. "I'm tired of being left behind. Besides, I think it's time that we stormed the kingdom for help." She stretched her hands to Dave on her left and Ace on her right. Together they formed a circle around the table. Donna prayed, "Lord, this little girl doesn't deserve what's happened to her. She's in trouble right now and needs your healing help. Please restore her to full health and strength. Also, Lord, please bring this whole business to an end so that this family can return to New Hampshire. These things we ask in Jesus' name."

Everyone said, "Amen."

"Getting a little bossy with the Boss, aren't you, Reverend?" Millie asked.

"Ask and you shall receive," Donna said. "I'm testing the promise."

"What about the New Hampshire part?"

"That got a little personal, didn't it?"

"Yep."

"Well, it's how I feel. I miss the Garrison's."

"We miss New Hampshire," Lauren said, squeezing Ace's hand.

"Will you stay here or come back?" Ace asked.

"Jury's out," Lauren said, "but I don't think Mark's committed to staying."

"I'm hungry," Millie said. "If we're going to the hospital, let's go."

"I'm not here as your enemy," I say. "I just want to express my sympathy to you and Lonnie."

"My husband's dead because you rangers killed him."

"Not you rangers, Lettie. I didn't shoot Emil, but he was threatening Sarah's life so Ranger Toussant did what he thought he had to do."

"Emil would never kill a little girl," Lettie says defiantly. It isn't the time to discuss Lovely and Beth.

"Perhaps not, we'll get the whole story soon enough. I just want to know if there's anything I can do for you and Lonnie."

"Just leave us alone."

"Okay." I start to leave, but Lonnie blocks my way.

"Ranger Garrison, would you call as soon as you know if Sarah's okay?" I look at Lettie. She's shaking her head slowly.

"Of course, Lonnie." Before I can step out of the door, Lettie stands up.

"Ranger Garrison, there's one thing I want to say before you leave. You can believe it or not, but it's the God's truth. Emil had dreams. He told me plenty of times that some day we would be able to afford a real house and have nice things. I think whatever he did he did it for Lonnie and me. One thing's for certain. He wasn't able to run no bootlegging operation as they say. He didn't have no education, but he was a good worker. I don't want him to take all the blame for the stuff that's happened, you understand?"

"I understand, Lettie."

"What's going to happen to us?" Her voice breaks and she turns away.

"I wish I could say, Lettie, but I can't. Lauren and I will help any way that we can."

"That's decent of you," Lettie says, "but I ain't gonna ask nothing of the people that killed Emil."

All I want to do when I leave Lachine's is go home and sleep, but the apartment is empty. Thinking I've missed a call from Lauren, I go into the kitchen to get a snack. A note on the counter reads, "We've all gone to the hospital. No word yet. Just couldn't stay here any longer. Get a nap. I'll call when we get some word. Lauren." I grab a banana and drive to the hospital. Everyone is waiting in the ICU lounge.

"No word, Mark," Dave says as I come into the lounge.

"Do they know we're here?" I ask.

"Yep," Lauren answers, standing and giving me a hug. "Sarah's holding her own, but she's still in a coma. Dr. Ward isn't here and no one will say anything more."

"Stay here," I say to Lauren then walk to the phone. The doors are opened and I go to the nurse's station.

"Mr. Garrison, we have nothing to tell you right now. Her treatment hasn't changed and she hasn't come out of her coma."

"What about her vital signs?"

"Stable."

"Is this taking longer than usual?"

"Yes, but a coma isn't a bad thing. It means that her body is functioning at its most efficient level."

"What exactly does that mean?"

"As long as her 'vital signs' as you call them are okay, her body is in a deep rest. You'll have to ask the doctor for more information. He'll be here shortly for rounds."

"Please tell him that we're here."

"He already knows."

"Thank you."

"Let's get breakfast," I say to the others in the lounge.

"Not so fast, Mark," Lauren says. "The Natchitoches sheriff called. He's scheduled a task force meeting for tomorrow at eight. I told him that unless he heard otherwise, you'd be there."

The meeting starts on time. Deputy Durand convenes from the head of an elliptical table and six padded chairs. A dry erase board is on a tripod to Durand's right. The names of the victims are written in the order of their event: Lovely Hampden and Beth Beckett, murdered at Bayou Pierre; Samuel Kirby and Franklin Fisch, murdered in a staged car wreck; Sarah Adams, kidnapped and poisoned; Mark Richards, murdered by Emil Lachine; Emil Lachine, shot by Ranger Toussant. I sit at the end of the table opposite Durand. To my left are Pete and the sheriff. To my right are agents of the ATF and Louisiana state police.

"Six people have died and Sarah Adams is in a coma, gentlemen," Durand says. "And we have one man in custody who's chirping like a bird. He admits complicity in the deaths of the Hampden and Beckett girls, the abduction and poisoning of Sarah Adams, and the production and distribution of untaxed liquor. He denies any involvement in the deaths of Kirby, Fisch, or Richards. He claims he witnessed the shooting of Richards by Constable Lachine. We know that Lachine was killed during the commission of a crime by Ranger Toussant. We have a common denominator here, gentlemen. Anyone want to guess what it is?"

"Alcohol," I say. "And these aren't the only incidents involving alcohol."

"Alcohol is certainly involved. All except Richards and Lachine were drunk or in an alcoholic coma when they died. Sarah Adams is still in an alcoholic coma. For the past year we've had a significant rise in the number of alcohol-related crimes in our parish and west of the state border, including incidents involving minors. I'm going to turn the meeting over to our ATF colleague from New Orleans."

The ATF agent gives a briefing on the mission of the organization and the work already being done in the parish. "The liquor and still are being destroyed as I speak and we're rounding up distributors identified by the man in the sheriff's custody. Our next effort will be to seize the assets of anyone connected with the illegal liquor production. We're doing everything necessary to shut down this operation."

Durand thanks the agent then repeats to the group what he's told me about Mitch's statement—that Emil wasn't calling the shots. "The man in custody has told us that Constable Lachine was not the top man in this bootlegging operation. He claims that Lachine was just following orders."

"What do we know about Lachine?" the state policeman asks.

"A town constable—kept order in Roberval. He was assisting Ranger Garrison in the investigations of the girls found in the Kisatchie, isn't that right, Garrison?"

"In a manner of speaking."

"Why was he assisting in a federal investigation?" the officer asks, turning to me.

"His assistance was requested by Ranger Toussant, my supervisor." All eyes turn to Toussant.

"Roberval is in close proximity to the forest. I thought he might be of assistance to Ranger Garrison, being new in town." That seems to satisfy the group.

Just as Durand is about to ask for a report from the state policeman about the auto deaths, there is a light tap on the conference room door. Durand walks to the door and receives a folded note from the clerk. He thanks her, closes the door and opens the note. "Ranger Garrison, will you step into the corridor, please." I leave quickly, expecting news about Sarah.

Dave is in the corridor. "Sarah's awake, Mark."

"Let's go," I say, starting down the hallway.

"It's not necessary, Mark. They're not letting us see her. She's not herself."

"I have to get to Lauren."

"Ace has taken her home. They've given her a sedative."

I step into the conference room. They've taken a break in my absence. "I'm going to have to leave. Sarah's awake," I say to Durand.

"Go, Toussant can bring you up to speed on what you miss."

CHAPTER 22

▼

Millie answers the door. "Lauren's in the bedroom. She may be asleep. They gave her some strong stuff."

"Thanks, Millie," I say, heading for the bedroom. Lauren's awake.

"Oh, Mark," she says, trying to stand up. I ease her down on the bed. "Easy, honey, you're a little wobbly."

"They gave me something, Mark. Sarah's not right. They wouldn't let me see her."

"What do you mean she's not right?"

"They wouldn't say right out, just that they want to observe her until tomorrow, then we can see her."

"Did they say anything?"

"She wasn't making any sense."

"Let's not panic. Dr. Ward said that it might take some time. I'm going to stay with you. Lay down while I speak to the others, then I'll come to bed. We all need a good rest."

"Mark, I hate to say this," Dave says, "but if Sarah's over the hurdle, we're going to have to return to New Hampshire. I got a call from my supervisor this afternoon. She's a bit over her head." Lauren's asleep when I return to the bedroom. I lay down next to her and watch her breathe. What have I put her through?

"I'm going to take her makeup, Mark," Lauren says as we rush to get ready to see Sarah.

"How about clothes?" I ask.

"She has what she needs."

"I didn't mention it yesterday, Lauren, but Dave and Donna will be flying back as soon as Sarah's out of the woods. He's needed on the Appalachian Trail."

"It's great that they could stay this long. When are they leaving?"

"I don't know for sure, but Donna's packing their things now."

We go to ICU and call the desk. "Sarah Adams has been moved to a step-down unit on the third floor, Mr. Garrison," the clerk says. I get directions and we walk quickly to the stairway. Arrow signs on the wall direct us to the nurse's station.

"We're Sarah Adams' parents," I tell the clerk. "We were told that we could see her today."

"We've been expecting you. Sarah's getting a sponge bath right now, but you're welcome to wait outside her room if you like."

She directs us to the room. The door is closed. Lauren peeks in and calls, "Everyone decent?"

"Come in, please," a young woman says. "We'll be back in thirty minutes to change Sarah's bedding, but you can visit with her now. She's in a chair."

Lauren bursts through the door and almost trips over a wastebasket. "Be careful, Mom," Sarah says, smiling softly.

"Oh, honey," Lauren says, reaching toward her daughter. She looks horrible, but she's alive. I try not to let my shock show on my face. She looks up at me over her mother's shoulder and smiles. I wave. Lauren is crying.

"How are you, sweetheart?" I ask.

"Not sure," she says slowly. "Can't get my head straight." Lauren sits on the edge of Sarah's bed. I study Sarah. She's lost weight, her skin is blotchy, but her eyes are clear. Someone has done a good job cleaning her up and grooming her hair. Several bags are hanging on the IV pole so I assume that she's being fed intravenously and receiving some medications. She sees me looking at the bags. "They say I was dehydrated and they're trying to get my fluids back to normal. The others are antibiotics and something for my headache."

"How bad is your headache, Sarah?" I ask.

"Don't have one right now."

"So it's working."

"Guess so."

"Are you strong enough to walk?" Lauren asks. Sarah smiles.

"Sure, but I don't feel like dancing." Lauren smiles. "They gave me some pudding today. It's the first real food I've had, if you can call pudding real food. They also took an order for my lunch. Looks like I'll get a real meal in awhile."

"Can I stay with you until lunch, or will that wear you out?"

"Please stay. I need to talk to someone other than the police." My ears perk up.

"You've talked to the police? Who? When?" I'm surprised and annoyed that the police had access to Sarah before her parents.

"Just before you got here. His card is on the table. He just wanted to know whether I would be willing to look at some pictures. I told him I would. He said he'd be back. He was very nice." I pick up Deputy Durand's card and put it in my pocket.

"Sarah, would you like me to do your nails and brush your hair? I also have your makeup kit."

"I'd love that, Mom. I've never felt as dirty as I did when I was ..." She doesn't finish the sentence. "I can't exactly remember everything. It's coming back slowly."

"You don't need to remember anything for me. When you're ready to remember and talk about it, I'll be here to listen. Mark, we're going to do some girl stuff. Do you want to stay?"

"Actually, I'd like to tell Dave and Donna that they can go back to New England. I may need to drive them to the airport. I'll get word to you." I kiss Sarah on the forehead and give Lauren a hug. "Be sure to make notes when you see the doctor," I say as I leave the room.

I call Dave from the lobby of the hospital. "Sarah's fine. What are your plans?"

"We're going to need a ride to the airport after I turn in our car. We're going to take our chances on standby."

"Are you packed and ready to go?"

"Yes."

"Why don't we meet at the car rental place? I can be there in five minutes."

"Let's meet at the hospital in half an hour. We want to say goodbye to Sarah and Lauren. We've already said goodbye to Ace and Millie, then we can make the switch at the car rental place."

"Done deal. I'm going to go down the street to see Durand for a minute. Sarah's in room 311 on the third floor. Lauren's with her now. I'll meet you in the hospital lobby in thirty minutes."

I get lucky. Durand is with the sheriff. He steps out of their meeting to ask about Sarah. "You should know the answer to that. I understand you've seen her this morning." It sounds accusatory, which it probably is. He doesn't flinch.

"Right now, she's our best witness, Mark."

"She's not ready to be a witness. I'm sure her memory will improve in a matter of days. In the meantime, how about giving her a little time?"

"I asked if she'd be willing to look at some pictures. She agreed. Do you have a problem with that?"

"No, but make sure Lauren's with her, please."

"That's fair."

"Any leads on who's at the top of the organization?"

"None, that's what I'm hoping to get from Sarah."

I walk from the station to the Ranger District office to let Pete know that I'll be taking Dave and Donna to the airport.

"I take it Sarah's okay," he says.

"For now. She's recovering her memory slowly."

"How much recall does she have?"

"It's coming back. Deputy Durand is hoping that she'll be able to help identify the person Lachine worked for. He's planning to do a photo lineup today, if possible. We'll see."

"Give Dave my thanks for his help. Tell him I hope Donna is fully recovered and that they have a safe trip home."

"Will do, and I'll check in when I get back from the airport."

I had kept Dave and Donna waiting at the hospital. He didn't have the key to the SUV so they had stacked their luggage in the hospital parking lot. I find Dave sitting on a suitcase and Donna leaning against the SUV. "Sorry, guys, I went to the Ranger District office to bring Pete up to speed on my discussion with Durand. Are you ready to return the car and head for the airport?"

"Not really," Donna says. "We'd much rather extend the vacation, but with Sarah on the mend it's hard to justify." We load their luggage and they follow me to the car rental office. They go through the express checkout and we head for Shreveport."

"Are you standing by for a specific flight, or just hoping to get something going your way?"

"There's a flight leaving for Logan in a couple of hours," Dave says. "If we make it, great. If not, we'll stand by for something going that direction." We swing on to I-49 and head north toward Shreveport Regional. The trip should take about an hour and fifteen minutes if traffic is moving.

"We review their vacation and talk about future visits. As we approach LA 526, the Shreveport bypass, my cell phone rings. It's Lauren.

▼ ————————

CHAPTER 23

"I'm so glad I got you, Mark. It's Pete," she says, obviously out of breath.

"What's Pete?"

"Pete is Lachine's boss." It takes a minute for that to sink in.

"Come on, Lauren, you're kidding."

"Sarah remembers his voice."

"Sarah remembers his voice from where?"

"She heard two men outside the bathroom at the Red Bluff Camp. Lachine came in and left food for her. The other person didn't come in; then after Lachine left she heard them arguing before they walked away. She didn't recognize the second voice until now. Pete sat next to Sarah at the church reception after Daddy's wedding, so she knew his voice. She's certain that Lachine was arguing with Pete."

"I'm coming back," I say.

"What about Dave and Donna?"

"They'll have to leave later. I just told Pete that Sarah is our key witness. I'm coming back. I'll meet you at the hospital. Tell Millie and Ace to stay at the apartment."

Dave can see the panic on my face. "What's up?" he asks.

"Sarah says that it was Pete who was talking with Lachine outside of the bathroom at Red Bluff. Pete's the key player we've been looking for. I've got to get to the hospital. I just told Pete that Sarah is Durand's key witness."

"Let's go. I can help." I get back on I-49 and head south. "If we get stopped for speeding, call Sheriff Hardman. Get a pass. I'm not stopping."

"Roger."

"Is she certain?" Donna asks.

"Sarah was certain."

"But wasn't she drunk?"

"Maybe, but we don't know how drunk. And fear is a great sobering agent. I'm sure she heard everything that happened outside that bathroom."

"What did we miss?" Dave asks. "How could we have been so blind?" I'm only half listening to my friends as I swerve in and out of traffic, wishing I was in my official vehicle with sirens blaring.

"I should have paid attention to my instincts, Dave. When Pete's fingerprints were identified on the gas can a bell rang in my head, but I turned it off. Repeatedly, he told me that he wasn't a fisherman. Why would he have handled that gas can? It was Pete who drilled holes in the boat and emptied the can. His prints had to have been fresh to have been identifiable on that old can."

"Is there anything else?" Donna asks, leaning forward and holding on to the back of the front seat.

"Yes, when the results came in from the test of Lovely's hair, he put them away in his desk. I had to ask for them. He said that he left a message on my answering machine at home, but I don't have an answering machine. Then when he gave me the results I went to copy them, but he told me that the copier was down. It wasn't—I looked when I left the office."

"What else?" Dave asks.

"When I asked him about the barn that you saw in the Kisatchie, Donna, he denied knowledge of the barn, but knew about your accident. It didn't fit then, and it doesn't fit now. How could I have been so stupid?"

"You trusted him," Dave says.

"More than I should have. I told him that I was going to take an official car and investigate the barn to see if anyone had information I could use in my investigation of the deaths at Bayou Pierre. Pete suddenly remembered that the vehicle was scheduled for service. Then on several occasions Pete tried to take me off of the investigation, claiming jurisdictional problems."

"Maybe this explains why no one searched the Red Bluff Camp," Dave says. "Didn't Pete assign the search routes?"

"Right, and Pete never told me about the death of Lovely Hampden. I found that out on my own. He took no active role in the investigation and as far as I could tell nothing had been done before I arrived."

"This explains why he and Lachine were so close. Actually, Mark, I wondered why Lachine was involved in the investigation at all. He was a low level enforcement officer in a small town, right?"

"Right, Pete put Lachine in my way to slow down the investigation."

"And to be able to maintain an inside track on your work."

"Wasn't it Pete who suggested that you go fishing?" Donna asks.

"Hello. Where was my mind? When I told him about the attempt to sink the boat, he dismissed it as inexperience on Toledo Bend and did nothing to pursue the investigation."

I was sick. I had missed every clue along the way. Now, Pete is in Natchitoches with easy access to the key witness, whom I identified.

"Did you bring any weapons?" Dave asks. I know where he's going with his question.

"No weapons, Dave. Not in the hospital. Please get Durand on the phone. I'll talk to him." I put on my headset and Dave plugs my phone into it. It's already ringing. Durand is out of the office. I tell them that it's an emergency and they agree to locate him. I keep the headset in place and stay the course on I-49. The return trip is taking considerably less time than the trip north. We're already turning on to LA 6 when Durand calls. I fill him in on what we suspect and ask him to meet me at the hospital with enough men to back me up.

"Back you up, hell," Durand says. "You're not going in, Mark. You're too close to this and out of your jurisdiction."

"Jurisdiction, hell," I say back. "I've heard too much talk about jurisdictions during the past months. This is my daughter. No one's going to stop me from making a dash to her room, Durand, and I'm going to get to the hospital before you do. I'm turning into the parking lot as we speak." I pull up to the main entrance, toss the headset, and dash through the lobby. Dave follows as Donna takes charge of the SUV. I can hear sirens on the street.

There are three people waiting for the up elevator. I dash around the corner to the staff elevator and see Dr. Ward waiting at the door. I open the door to the stairwell and double step the stairs. I nearly knock a food cart over opening the door onto the third floor. Room 311 is past the nurse's station. As I run past, a nurse shouts after me, "Mr. Garrison, you can't go in there. The doctor is with your daughter." If that's true, the doctor's in two places at the same time. The door to Sarah's room is closed.

Just as I'm ready to burst into the room, Dave, Durand, and two of his deputies step out of the elevator. I open Sarah's door and see a man in hospital scrubs standing over Sarah's bed with his back to the door. He's holding a pillow over Sarah's face. At the sound of the door opening, Pete turns to face me. From under his scrubs, he pulls out his service weapon.

"You son-of-a-bitch," I say. "I trusted you."

"Your problem, Mark," Pete says as he points the gun at my head. "Move to the other side of the bed."

I begin to follow his advice. Just as I do, all hell breaks loose. Dave bursts through the door. Pete turns to look, and as he does terror and rage coalesce in Sarah, and with the swiftness and strength of a puma, she slams the edge of her food tray into Toussant's forearm. He screams as radius and tray crunch simultaneously, releasing the gun from his hand. The weapon falls and slides across the polished floor toward the door. Dave and I dive for Pete from opposite directions. I ram my knee into his groin and he doubles over as Dave, five inches shorter but built like a bear, catches him with an uppercut. Toussant's jaw goes the way of his radius and he collapses to the floor face down.

Durand, watching the scuffle from the door, slaps a set of cuffs on him. Two deputies hoist him to his feet and drag him out of the room.

Sarah's sobbing and shaking. She reaches up and lets me hold her. "Get a nurse, quickly," I say to Dave, "then find Lauren, please." Staff members are taking emergency precautions by moving patients out of adjoining rooms. A nurse comes rushing into Sarah's room and attends to her. I step into the corridor in time to intercept Lauren. "They're settling Sarah down, but you should go in to her."

"The ME is in the hospital, Mark. He's on his way up," Durand says. "He'll need to seal the room. Let's see if they can get Sarah out of here." In fact, the nurses are already looking for another room, but Dr. Ward decides to release her instead.

"She's ready for home care, Mr. Garrison," the doctor says. "She's going to need a different kind of help than I can provide. I'll give you a referral for her to see a counselor and a neurologist."

"Make sure they're close to Woodsville, New Hampshire," I say.

Sarah Is helped to a wheelchair and rolled out of room 311. She never looks back. Lauren quickly packs Sarah's things into a plastic bag and we all walk quickly to a conference room at the end of the corridor and wait for Dr. Ward to arrange for her release. Sarah's head is on her mother's shoulder. Both sit silently while I speak quietly with Durand. Dave leaves to bring the SUV to the front of the hospital to take us home.

"I'll need your statement, Mark."

"When will we be free to return to New England?"

"It'll take a few days to get everything in order, Mark. You know how these things work."

"We'll make arrangements for the move. I can't thank you enough for your support through all of this."

"It's part of the job, Mark. You've helped us clear up a real mess. I owe you thanks." We shake hands.

A nurse comes into the conference room to review discharge papers for Sarah. She will obtain Sarah's medical records and coordinate Sarah's care with a physician in New Hampshire. Two prescriptions are handed to Lauren and we're dismissed. The nurse pushes Sarah's wheelchair to the SUV and helps her into the vehicle. Donna and Lauren sit in the back with Sarah. Dave follows in Ace's convertible.

Millie, Ace, and Lonnie are at the apartment when we arrive. Two flower arrangements are in Sarah's room with a "Welcome home, Sarah" note written on her wall mirror with lipstick, but Sarah's already asleep. I carry her to her bed and Lauren lies down with her. The rest of us collapse into chairs in the living room.

CHAPTER 24

▼

The first thing Sarah said after sleeping fourteen hours was, "Can we go home now?"

"Honey, we're going to go home," Lauren answered.

"I mean home to New Hampshire."

"So do I, just as soon as Mark wraps up the legal stuff."

"Mom, did I hurt a man in the hospital or did I dream that?"

"It isn't important right now, Sarah."

"It's important to me."

"Yes, you defended yourself against a man who was trying to kill you."

"Do you think God can forgive me for that?"

"He already has."

"Mom, did Mark save my life?"

"He sure did."

"Is Grandpa here?"

"He's been sleeping in a chair in the living room since you came home from the hospital. Would you like to see him?"

"Uh huh"

"I'll get him. Is there anything you want from the kitchen?"

"Lots of things, but first I'd like to talk to Grandpa."

"Hi, sweetheart," Ace said.

"Hi, Grandpa."

"Can I sit on the bed?"

"Sure. Grandpa?"

"What, honey?"

"Did you know my real father?"

"No."

"Really?"

"Really. Why are you asking about him?"

"I wish Mark were my real father."

"What is a father?"

"You know."

"Besides that, what is a father?"

"Someone who takes care of you."

"Does Mark take care of you?"

"He takes care of Mom and me."

"Does he love you?"

"He says he does."

"Do you believe him?"

"Yes."

"Do you love him?"

"I don't know how, Grandpa. I want to love him, but I don't know how to start, or what to say."

"What do you say to me all the time?"

"I love you, Grandpa."

"Now, try it, but substitute Mark for Grandpa." Sarah smiled.

"I get it."

"No, try it."

"I love you, Mark."

"Now, how hard was that?"

"You can go now, Grandpa," Sarah said, sitting up and hugging Ace. He held his tears until Sarah's head was on his shoulder.

It takes two and one-half hours to finish the paperwork, but when we're done Durand has all he needs. "I'll call you in New Hampshire if we need you to testify, Mark, but I think this thing is going to drag on for months. I'm sure we can get your information by deposition. I can't speak for the federal agencies, but as far as the deaths are concerned, the bad guys are dead or in custody, and Sarah's assault on Toussant was clearly in self defense. I just hope you won't remember Louisiana badly. There are really good people here. Now that you've shut down the bootlegging, we'll be a better place. We need people like you, Mark. If you ever get bored with those law-abiding folks in New England, think seriously about coming down here. We need someone who walks tall to keep us in line."

He walks me to the door. "I'd offer to buy you a drink, Mark, but I'm sure you want to get home to your family."

"Durand, they're darned lucky to have you in place. Keep up the good work. Who knows—maybe our paths will cross again."

I drive home. For the first time I feel as though my work is done. I don't know what the Forest Service will do without a supervisor at the Kisatchie Ranger District, but, frankly, I don't care. I'll deal with the Forest Service tomorrow. Now, I want to hold my wife and daughter.

When I get home, Millie and Ace are in the kitchen with Lauren. Dave and Donna are waiting for Ace to take them to the airport. Lonnie is hanging around hoping to see Sarah. I hug Dave and Donna and promise to share experiences when we get back to New Hampshire.

"Mark, I believe Sarah's awake," Lauren says. "Would you like to go in and see her?"

"Yes."

"Hi, Daddy," she says when I walk through the door. She swings her legs to the floor and tries to stand, but is unsteady. I grab her before she falls and ease her back down on the bed. "Sorry," she says.

"Don't be sorry, honey. You'll get your strength back."

"I wish I could get my memory back."

"God has a way of protecting us when we've been hurt, Sarah. He blanks things out until we're ready to handle them."

"Do you think God was protecting me when I was alone?"

"You're here, aren't you?" She nods.

"Daddy, I want to say something."

"I'm right here."

"I love you, and I want you to be my father." I melt down. It's more than I can handle. I sit down on the bed, lower my head into my hands and let it all pour out. Sarah moves next to me and takes my hand without saying a word. I'm beyond embarrassment or manly pride. We are one in spirit.

"I love you, too, Sarah, and I want to be your father. Deal?"

"Deal."

It's ten when Ace returns from the airport. "Get the ranger and minister home?" I ask.

"Got them started," Ace says. "Now it's our turn to leave."

"We were on our honeymoon, or has everyone forgotten about that?" Millie says. "It took me over a year to get this old man in a romantic mood. Think you can leave us alone for a week or so?" We laugh with Millie. "Let's toss our stuff in the convertible and try again, Ace."

"You mean tonight?"

"I mean right after breakfast in the morning. Then we'll take our sweet time in New Orleans before we head back. Can we move into Dave and Donna's room for the night?"

"You bet," Lauren says.

The Supervisor of the Kisatchie National Forest in Louisiana is located in Pineville, near Alexandria. It takes exactly three and a half hours to get to my appointment with Toussant's boss. All he knows about the situation in our district is what he's been told by the other federal agents. Pete effectively covered his tracks. I wonder whether the supervisor will ask me to stay until Pete's position is filled. He doesn't even mention it, suggesting instead that I return to my home base in New Hampshire and take a one-month leave with pay. I'll be recommended for a commendation and promotion for my part in the investigation of the death of Beth Beckett. My next assignment will come down before my leave ends.

I leave our six-hour meeting feeling affirmed and free to begin a delayed honeymoon. I call Lauren on the way home and share the good news. Ace and Millie have decided to stay another day and are at the apartment when I return. A gigantic house-swap is in the works. Ace had been planning to move into the farm house that Millie occupies. It's part of a farm that I bought from Millie before I was transferred to Louisiana. Instead, they decide to live in Ace's ranch house, a much smaller home, but more manageable for folks their age. Lauren, Sarah, and I will move into the farm house. To my surprise, Lauren has arranged for Lettie and Lonnie Lachine to sublease our apartment in Natchitoches until they can sell their trailer and find a house or apartment of their own. The town of Roberval had a generous life insurance policy on Emil that he never mentioned. He kept his promise to Lettie that he would "make it big" someday.

We watch Millie and Ace leave for New Orleans in their Mustang convertible. "We're turning off our cell phones," Millie yells from the street, giving us a Queen Elizabeth wave. Lonnie is in the kitchen playing backgammon with Sarah when Lauren and I return to the house.

"Would it be all right if I take Sarah to a movie, Ranger Garrison?" Lauren looks at me with a wrinkled brow.

"We'll discuss it and let you know in a few minutes, Lonnie." I take Lauren for a walk, anticipating what she'll say.

"Are you feeling what I feel?" she asks, taking my hand.

"You're afraid to let Sarah out of your sight?"

"Exactly."

"It might be good for her to get her mind off of things."

"It hasn't been a week, Mark."

"Who's afraid, Sarah or us?"

"Me, I guess."

"Besides, I'd like some private time with you, Lauren." We agree to let the kids go to the movies as long as the picture is something light, and they agree to return immediately afterwards.

"We thought we'd get ice cream after the movie, okay?"

"Okay."

"Are you afraid that something will happen to me, Mom?"

"Would you blame me?"

"No, but I want to show you something." She lifts her left hand for Lauren to see. "See this ring? It's the ring Millie gave me. Whenever I was afraid, Mom, I did two things. First, I prayed that God would help me. Second, I thought about my ring and everything that's happened to Millie during her life. You've called her a survivor and I had her ring. That makes me a survivor, too. God and Millie give me strength. They're always with me."

"I love you, Sarah."

"I love you, too, Mom."

The youngsters leave in Lonnie's new older car. We sit in the kitchen and watch them.

"Do you really believe that God helped Sarah, Mark?"

"She's okay, right?"

"Right."

"We're alone," I say to Lauren.

"How long has it been?"

"A century?"

"Do we have any wine?"

"Maybe," Lauren says as she reaches into a kitchen cabinet for a bottle of white Port. I pour two glasses and take my bride by the hand into the living room. We sit together on the couch without saying a word. When the glasses are empty, we walk to the bedroom.

Little by little Sarah's memory of our Louisiana sojourn returns and she reveals amazing things about beatings, naked captivity, pumas, escapes, and the smell of a still. We weep together, pray together, and bond in unforgettable ways.

We return the way we came, by way of the Natchez Trace Parkway. As we cross the Mississippi River into Natchez, Sarah calls out from the back seat, "Hey, you guys, could we get some of that coconut pie at Mammy's Cupboard?"

"Her memory's back," Lauren says.

978-0-595-44418-2
0-595-44418-0

Printed in the United States
77738LV00005B/31-60

9 780595 444182